ZANE PRESENTS

Twisted
Entrapment

Dear Reader:

N'Tyse is back with her own brand of deception and erotica with the third novel in her *Twisted* series. The author's titles feature characters with twisted actions and minds. From a woman who's faked her own death to a couple who's lost everything and life's a scandal, this action-packed drama keeps readers guessing what will happen next.

If you haven't read this author's works, prepare for a thrilling ride as secrets are revealed, relationships are challenged, and obsession flourishes. An excerpt from the first title, *Twisted Seduction*, is included in the back. The second installment is *Twisted Vows of Seduction*.

Following the story, N'Tyse promotes HIV awareness with statistics and resources and how it affects specific communities.

As always, thanks for supporting myself and the Strebor Books family. We strive to bring you the most cutting-edge, out-of-the-box material on the market. You can find me on Facebook @AuthorZane or you can email me at zane@eroticanoir.com.

Blessings,

Zane

Publisher
Strebor Books
www.simonandschuster.com

ALSO BY N'TYSE
Gutta Mamis
Twisted Vows of Seduction
Twisted Seduction

ZANE PRESENTS

TWISTED
Entrapment

A NOVEL

N'TYSE

SBI

STREBOR BOOKS

NEW YORK LONDON TORONTO SYDNEY

Strebor Books
P.O. Box 6505
Largo, MD 20792
http://www.streborbooks.com

ISBN 978-1-59309-614-4
ISBN 978-1-4767-8294-2 (ebook)
LCCN 2015934630

First Strebor Books trade paperback edition July 2015

Cover design: www.mariondesigns.com
Cover photograph: © Keith Saunders/Keith Saunders Photos

10 9 8 7 6 5 4 3 2 1

Manufactured in the United States of America

For information regarding special discounts for bulk purchases, please contact Simon & Schuster Special Sales at 1-866-506-1949

The Simon & Schuster Speakers Bureau can bring authors to your live event. For more information or to book an event, contact the Simon & Schuster Speakers Bureau at 1-866-248-3049 or visit our website at www.simonspeakers.com.

Dedicated to all the twisted folks here and abroad.
Including those in denial.

"The most important ingredient we put into any relationship is not what we say or what we do, but what we are."

—STEPHEN R. COVEY

Acknowledgments

This book by far is one of the hardest books I have ever had to write. Let me just go on and put that out there. I had a major production going on in my belly that required more beauty rest than normal. So you must know how relieved and excited I am to have reached this point. As I write this, I am seven weeks away from giving birth to my prince, Zamari. Many nights when I'm up working and hubby and daughter are asleep, I begin to count my blessings. I am truly blessed for the opportunity God has granted me to do what I love, and I am humbly grateful for the platform I've been given to share my passion and wild twisted stories with the world. I want to take the time to acknowledge those that made it possible.

First and foremost, Zane. You have not only been a great mentor, but one of the best publishers in America that I have the pleasure of working with. I can't thank you enough for always keeping it real. Charmaine, you are THE BEST in the business. You've been so understanding throughout the labor of this project and while I know you have a hundred other authors to tend to, you've always managed to check in on me. That made me feel special. To my loving husband and beautiful baby girl, you are the wind beneath my wings. With you two by my side, I can do anything I set my mind to. I love you both with all my heart.

To my immediate literary family and friends, I love you guys!

Vanessa Morman, Anna Black, Sincere, Shakir Rashaan, Leiann B. Wrytes, Sh'Moore, Candy Hall, Martin Soli Roy, Johnathan Royal, Victoria Jones, Raynesha Pittman, Layla Rashaan, Brandie Davis, Fabiola Joseph, Tiffany Tyler, Dock Bookshop, Book Referees, OOSA Book Club, Sista 2 Sista Book Club, Strebor, Our Black Is Beautiful Book Club, Sistahs of Essence, AAMBC, Urban Reviews, and all of you who continue to support me and my endeavors. There are way too many to name, but please know you are appreciated.

What's next you ask? As I wrap up this project I am preparing to dive into the final installment in this Twisted series, so please be on the lookout. Also, if you have not heard, I executively produced and directed my first independent docu-film entitled *Beneath My Skin*. Please check it out and let me know what you think. Until next time, don't be a stranger. Join me on Facebook and Twitter. I love chatting with fellow writers and readers. ☺

The Setup

"I can't believe I actually agreed to go through with this! What in the hell was I thinking?"

Sabrina Montgomery stared vacuously into thin air as she mentally played out the twisted avocation. Her smooth, golden-peach skin shimmered, and her long, lustrous, black mane contoured her bare face, sheltering the most pronounced feature on her body. If it weren't for the slightest chill of air that invaded her space, the double chocolate morsels protruding from her perfectly round, ample flesh would have otherwise remained shrouded behind their silk curtains. Hazel-green irises that usually sat boldly behind deep-set eyes were suddenly blanketed with looming discontent.

Initially, she had been repulsed and offended by the idea her husband had proposed four months earlier. She had thought he'd lost his fucking mind. And for the first time in their six years of marriage, she questioned if he loved her anymore; if he had suddenly become unfaithful; if their circumstances had grown so unbearable that he would rather push her into another man's arms than sit around and wait for her to up and leave him—making good on past threats. She questioned everything there was to question about Luke and their tainted nuptials, right up to this very testy moment.

Her sullen mood must have intimidated him, because for a man who spoke three languages and loved to dine in conversation, morning, noon and night, surprisingly, he didn't have one damn word to churn out. The more she contemplated over the situation, the heavier her conscience weighed in on Luke's sick, twisted motives. What kind of husband would permit his wife to have sex with another man, on his watch, in an attempt to get pregnant? It stood to reason that their tumultuous marriage had undoubtedly caused Luke's heart to stray, leaving Sabrina alone, cold, and blinded by the darkness.

Yes, their deteriorating marriage had seemingly reached a dead end, and while Sabrina was *trying* to salvage it, she had her reservations. When they had lost their son, Avery, their entire world came crashing down shortly thereafter. It was one horrible event after another. Luke lost his $250,000 insurance sales job after a major freak accident that ultimately revealed cocaine in his system. She had begged him to stop using long before his job found out, but he said it was the only thing that helped him get through the days. Needless to say, that unexpected blow drove them right into financial suicide. They seemingly went bankrupt overnight, and her world, as she knew it, slowly crumbled before her very eyes.

Still, Sabrina knew well enough that having another baby would not change what had already happened, nor would it replace the child they had lost. She couldn't help being bothered by Luke's indifference. Had they become so desperate to have another baby of their own that they were willing to rob a man of his sperm to get it? She shuddered at the thought. As much as she would have liked to fulfill Luke's wish, she could only imagine the disappointment and regret they would feel if this thing backfired. That hunch alone was enough motivation for her to back out while she still had the chance.

The irony in it all was that she had actually grown content with the way things were, accepting the verity that they may never experience parenthood again. She had been cheated out of motherhood three years ago, the day before their son, Avery, turned one years old. She had gone into his room to check on him at the same hour she had every morning, only that day, he didn't wake from his sleep. He had died suddenly and without explanation. Doctors called it SIDS (Sudden Infant Death Syndrome), but Sabrina called it God's way of getting even with her for aborting her twins when she was sixteen.

She and Luke had both fallen into a major depression after the loss of Avery. He was their everything, including the glue that kept their marriage strong. His death had put such a strain on their marriage that they began to drift further apart, until it felt as though they were merely roommates, hiding behind their own misery and unhappiness. Existing, yet invisible to one another. The devastation and grief that she alone experienced was beyond comprehension. No one seemed to understand what she was going through, not even her husband, who had unknowingly cornered her in that living Hell. It was impossible to be in the same room with one another without quarreling, so not speaking at all became their tacit agreement. It was easier to *deal* that way. But the isolation only fueled their tension, slowly disconnecting their only palpable communication line.

Sabrina tried to keep her head together and move past it the best way she knew how. That was *then*, this was *now*. She tried to convince herself that if she played along, if she seduced and milked this man for his semen the way her husband had coerced her, maybe, just maybe, things would go back to the way they were, long before tragedy, bullshit and bad luck intercepted their lives. Yet her reluctance wouldn't allow her to get past the what-ifs.

"What are we going to do if this entire thing blows up in our faces…or if it doesn't go according to plan, huh? Surely you have it all figured out, so please enlighten me on *that*," she sneered.

Luke deserted her concerns and upheld his silence. Before she knew it, her expression warped into an agonizing scowl, and her forehead crinkled as it always did when he pissed her off and challenged her mood.

As difficult as it was, she held back her tongue. Her eyes darted around the lofty master bedroom and its old-fashioned floral décor and heavenly white and gold Victorian-style furniture. The elderly, well-off white woman who had lived there for many years before them, had left the home in impeccable condition. It was beautiful and more than the Montgomerys could have ever afforded during their financial adversity. Besides a few minor modifications, everything was still in its place, exactly as Ms. Rester had left it, and as though she had never departed this life. Other than the understanding that she had no family or friends, they didn't know much about her or the four-thousand-square-foot property they'd illegitimately inherited over a year ago.

They had been squatters ever since the bank foreclosed on their house, hopping from one abandoned property to the next—mostly relinquished residential homes or foreclosures in affluent neighborhoods, well preserved by those allergic to misfortune but who had fallen on unexpected hard times, or in Ms. Rester's case, went home to Glory. The property had seemed to be a blessing, given that they'd been able to stay under the police officials' radar for as long as they had.

Sabrina inhaled sharply. The reality of their situation crashed down on her all at once. They were homeless, bankrupt, and one argument away from chunking their vows into the sewage. As if that wasn't enough connubial mayhem to sort through, she had to lend some common sense to her husband that supported why getting pregnant by a man she barely knew, was *not* the solution to their dysfunctional marriage.

"My gut is telling me we need to rethink this. Everything!" she retorted, coming to her senses and realizing how this could bring more harm than good. "It's just not right."

"Relax, Sabrina. You're overthinking things again." It was the first time Luke had said more than three words to her since being in her presence. "You have nothing to worry about." He slowly raised his head from the computer screen, his eyes seemingly refusing him in his attempt to connect with her. His vanilla-tanned skin reflected a warm hue of caramel that defined his lean and toned physique. His handsome chiseled face revealed a more pronounced jawline and his fairly thin lips curled into a comforting smile. "Like I told you before," he said, finally giving her full eye contact. "We're gonna rock his world to a Jane Taylor lullaby. Trust me on this. He'll enjoy *every* second of it," he added with disturbing confidence. The only reason he didn't see the look she'd just given him was because he immediately reverted his attention to whatever it was that had obviously proved to be more important than her right now.

Seated on the edge of the bed with her backside slightly gracing the cold headboard, Sabrina crossed one long and toned shapely leg over the other, exposing the delicate, sheer black lace of her panty line. She huffed in both anger and regret. Her leg shook violently as her anxiety levels instantly peaked. She was horny and pissed off. Not a good combination. Nostrils flared, Sabrina was fuming inside and her husband was too blind to notice. She needed a cigarette, a Valium, anything to calm the mental fits of delirium.

"My purse," she snapped, pointing to the luxurious leather handbag next to Luke. The one he had given her when they were experiencing happier times; when they weren't robbing and swindling innocent people, including the dead.

Luke stopped pecking at the keyboard all at once. Those chestnut brown eyes she fell in love with the first day they'd met, conjured up joyful memories but failed to sidetrack her thoughts completely. He turned to his side, scooped up the purse and passed it to her. A flirty grin flashed across his face in a weak attempt to get some kind of reaction out of her. Sabrina wasn't falling for it. This was serious business and it was about time he treated it as such, although he always said she was so damn sexy when she was mad. Perhaps it was that he simply could not resist her sexual allure.

"Thanks," she responded dryly. She fumbled inside for her cigarette case, slipped one out of the pack and fired it up. She could feel his eyes climbing her half-naked flesh. To placate her curiosity, she tilted her head, contorted her lips and channeled the smoke in the opposite direction. The shift in movement forced her hair to slide off her sun-kissed shoulders, leaving her delectably aroused breasts perfectly angled for her husband to scope out at his convenience. The premeditated gesture seemed to work in her favor. She had his full attention.

Luke lustfully swept his tongue across his lower lip. "So fucking sexy!"

"Don't try to change the subject," Sabrina chided. She inhaled the cigarette again and this time tilted her head and blew the smoke upward.

"Can't a man relish in his wife's beauty without being reprimanded?" He cocked his head to the side. "Seems I've worked up quite an appetite. Any suggestions?" She turned to her right in time to witness the horny glint in his eyes. Immediately her pussy became aroused at the thought of his tongue forcing its way past the gates of her sacred garden, but she was too damn stubborn to answer the call. The sweet coconut scent that poured from her skin, clashed with her cigarette, yet it didn't seem to interfere with Luke's newfound concentration.

"We seriously need to discuss this baby situation," she said, getting back to the matter at hand.

Luke exhaled sharply. "What more is there to talk about, Sabrina?" His brows furrowed with confusion.

"Money! Where are we going to get the money to take care of a baby? Or did you somehow forget that *technically* we're homeless and barely scraping by?"

"How can I forget? You feel the need to remind me every fucking day! It's not like I haven't been trying to get us out of this mess!"

She lowered her voice, dreading where this was headed. "I know you've been trying—"

"Well then, stop rubbing it in my face, for God's sake." Luke turned several shades of red in less than a minute.

"Look, all I'm trying to do…is point out…the *fact* that we're not in a position to expand our family right now. It takes money!"

"Let *me* worry about the money. You handle your end of the bargain."

Sabrina sighed heavily. She took another puff of her cigarette, trying her best to calm her nerves. After losing Avery, she had not even dreamt about having another baby. The topic never even surfaced until after Luke's freak accident. She still did not entertain the idea too much at that time because it wasn't like they had the money or the health insurance to afford artificial insemination, nor were they stable enough to meet adoption requirements. Things took a turn four months ago, the second they latched their sights on the tall, chiseled and debonair Jeff Jackson.

It was a Friday evening and Sabrina had been ambling the chip aisle of their neighborhood grocery store. She had walked around his parked shopping cart, dipped her knees slightly to grab a bag of her favorite chocolate-covered pretzels, and pretended she didn't feel him air kiss her round, taut ass with those scrumptious mahogany lips. They locked eyes immediately. She had presumed it was his daughter traipsing alongside him and his small son wrapped in his grip. She fancied in his appraisal of her sexiness before settling her curious gaze on his ring-less finger. The smile on her face stretched in appreciation and he meddled in her delight by saying, "I see somebody's got a sweet tooth." It was an awkward, innocuous moment; however, the sexual fervor mounting between them nearly brought her to climax. Her imagination took her places it had never taken her before, forcing her to neglect her usual modest behavior.

She had tried diverting her attention to avoid being caught with her hands in the cookie jar, but it was too late. Directly behind the man who had voluntarily stirred a conversation between her thighs, stood her husband, whom she hadn't seen come down the aisle. The quiet and numb look on his face declared his witness to the flirtatious flutter in her eyes and smile, the new beat in her step, and the sway of her ass clamoring for attention, yet he said nothing. Her body had betrayed her before she could even realize how she had conveniently exposed herself to another man. Her absent two-karat diamond wedding ring only made matters more beguiling. Yes, she was unhappily married, but married nonetheless. And her only testament to that truth had been twenty-six miles away, tucked in a pawnshop's vault. Luke had pawned the ring, along with other jewelry, the same day the bank foreclosed on their multimillion-dollar home.

After the encounter with Jeff, Luke devised his new scheme. Against her wishes, they followed him all the way home, which happened to be only two blocks over from Ms. Rester's house. Luke spied on Jeff for four months, monitoring his comings and goings like clockwork. He had practically discovered everything there was to know about their prospective donor, and what he couldn't dig up in public records or on the Internet, he managed to extract from Jeff's nosey neighbors whom Luke had befriended right away. Born with a gift for gab, Luke had deluded them all by having them believe he was a private investor looking to acquire several properties in the area, in addition to Ms. Rester's home. Before long, Jeff's name managed to worm its way into conversations. Apparently, he had been wanting to sell his house after losing his wife in a fatal car accident. That diminutive supply of insight only fueled Luke's illusive plan.

Breaking her train of thought, Sabrina's sorrowful eyes landed on Luke. She closed and reopened them. "I don't want to do it," she admitted finally. "I can't."

Luke stared at her blankly.

"Come on, sweetheart! We've gone over this a million times. You're making this more difficult than it has to be." He jumped up from the chaise. "What about our family? Or is that even mildly of importance to you anymore since your six-figure security blanket has been snatched from underneath you!"

She widened her eyes in both upset and disbelief. "You know damn well I never married you for your *money!*"

"Psst! You know what, Sabrina…one day I may start to believe that."

His insensitive remark was like a powerful kick to her gullet. She shook her head, squinting her eyes at the man she'd married. "Un… fucking…believable." She roughly pulled the cigarette back into her mouth, breathing heavily. When he turned his back to her, she inconspicuously slid her eyes back in his direction.

Luke snatched off his tie, cuff links, dress shirt and pants. He tossed each article of clothing over the back end of the chaise. He'd worn the ensemble to a job fair and had landed several interviews. Coupled with his good looks, professional candor and intellect, Luke was the perfect candidate, but like his past efforts, Sabrina knew today was all in vain. His checkered employment record and the unspeakable amount of debt they were in was plastered on his credit report, jeopardizing any real potential job offer. Surviving off her part-time income as a dance teacher at a nearby private school, they were barely getting by and making ends meet. The tables had turned and it was Sabrina seeing to it that they had food in their mouths. She had done everything in her power to keep them afloat, but it wasn't enough.

There was an eerie silence before their eyes finally met in the large quatrefoil-shape mirror. No matter how tough she tried to be, this was breaking her soul. She hated fighting with Luke, especially after all they'd been through. Why did he always have to question her morality? A duo of hot tears skid like a landslide down her face. How could he still believe that she had only married him for his money? Her head drifted forward until her two finger-tips dug into her left temple. Rings of white smoke encircled the air as she allowed their thoughts to mate. She sprouted from the bed, and then headed for the bathroom to shed her emotions in private.

Luke immediately grabbed her wrist once she stepped into his path. He plucked the remnant of the cigarette from between her fingers and mashed it in the ashtray on the dresser behind them. She pulled away from his embrace and he drew her right back in. With both his thumbs, he erased the tears running from her grief-stricken eyes. The gentleness of his touch brought them to one accord.

"I'm sorry," Luke said. He slid his finger down the right side of her cheek and glided it along her lips before slightly raising her chin and kissing her. Even with everything that had transpired, her body couldn't deny how good it felt to be touched and desired.

She closed her eyes briefly to bathe in his affections, instantly forgiving him. He interrupted their kiss and held her gaze. "I hate when we fight." He sighed heavily. "Before we know it, this will all be behind us. We'll get back to that place," he said promisingly. The sincerity laced in his voice and the electricity wired in his touch, made it all worth fighting for. "Trust me. Please. That's all I ask," Luke pleaded softly.

Her lips curved fairly into a smile as more tears rounded her chin. "I have faith that things will get better for us." The words barely crawled out of her mouth. "I...need you to realize that I fell in love with *you*. Not your money," she declared, looking him straight in the eyes. "Rest assured that if I was that type of woman, I would have tore my ass when it all dried up," she told him truthfully, no longer able to hide behind her emotions.

Luke mustered a smile. "I love you."

"I love you, too."

That simple exchange led to a kiss so erotically passionate that nothing else really mattered in that moment. A sensual moan squeezed through Sabrina's lips when his hand slipped inside her panties. His fingers eagerly examined her pool of excitement. Meeting his approval, he ripped off her underwear and tossed them to the floor. He wheeled his hands over her curvaceous ass, kissing and nibbling on her neck, her shoulder, and her round firm breasts.

They staggered back toward the bed, plopping onto it. He continued polishing her mounds, tugging at her nipples as if they were pieces of his favorite jerk chicken. Her guttural moans echoed off her tongue, the walls, and the vaulted ceilings throughout the house. She pulled his body closely into hers. Her legs drifted apart and his large hands glided along her warm brown thighs while his lips and tongue swirled around her burgeoning nipples. She hooked both of her legs over his sturdy shoulders, wanting nothing more right now than for him to bathe his tongue deeply inside of her pussy and make her cum.

Luke lowered his mouth to her middle and lapped up her sweet nectar as if it were Thanksgiving. She writhed feverishly in response, her pussy pouring in satisfaction from his caress.

"Oooooh, baby!" she panted. He dragged his warm wet tongue over and around her blossomed carnation until she was ready to surrender. When he had enough fun devouring her sunny-side up, he deftly flipped her over, impatiently took her back into his mouth, and baptized his face in her sweet, sticky dew all over again.

Sabrina closed her eyes and suctioned him deeper into her orifice, riding his tongue backward in record-breaking speed. He cupped one of her breasts and massaged her nipple simultaneously.

"I'm cumming," she cried in a sexual fit as his tongue went deep-sea fishing. She bucked her hips until her climax vengefully ripped through her pussy, causing a chain reaction. Her body quaked from the top of her head to the tips of her toes.

Feeling as though all of her energy had just been zapped out of her, she slowly rolled over on her back. Her chocolate morsels stood irresistibly erect and Luke rushed to their beck and call. He massaged her fleshy nipples between his teeth while caressing her beautiful body. He paused briefly and reached under the bed. He pulled out the black velvet treasure box and opened it. Sabrina watched wantonly as he strapped on the harness and the eight-inch black rubber dildo, surprised that he settled for that one instead of one of the others in his impressive collection.

He climbed back on top of her, bringing his appendage of choice to her lips. She rose to her elbows and gladly accepted his nightstick into her mouth, remembering precisely how sweet and salty his pre-cum used to taste. A delightful moan reverberated off her tongue, and as if he could actually *feel* her lips wrapped around his girth, he fervidly pumped her mouth, moaning satisfactorily. Once he was drizzled with her saliva, he gradually withdrew.

"Bend over," Luke instructed. He was in full control.

Sabrina obliged. She weakly climbed back on all fours and hiked her ass in midair, spreading her juicy, plumped lips. He kissed her ample bottom before entering her.

"Ooooooh!" she moaned, tugging at the bed sheets. "You feel so good."

Technology was simply amazing. Although silicon could never compete with real flesh, it definitely came close enough to curtail her sexual appetite. Luke made love to her relentlessly, going for as long as she needed him to, until *she* was satisfied.

After making love, he removed all the sex gear and joined her at the head of the bed. It was rare that he ever allowed her to see him this naked and without his attachment. It had taken him a while to even agree to the idea of using sex toys—he was too embarrassed. Luckily, he eventually came around to the idea his therapist had suggested. Sabrina hated this had to happen to him. She wished there had been a way to reverse his injury, but there wasn't. The motorcycle accident had happened months before they moved into Ms. Rester's home. The injury had been so bad, it severed his penis. Doctors had said that if the paramedics hadn't arrived when they had, he would have bled to death. They immediately performed surgery to reattach the blood vessels and other tissue, to no avail, leaving Luke with a one-inch stump and a complete loss of penile functions. Their marriage had already been suffering since the death of their son and the result of the accident had only complicated matters. It was like adding gasoline to the embers of an already faltering marriage.

Luke planted another loving kiss on her lips. He stared at her for a moment. "Promise me that we're in this together. That you want this baby just as bad as I do. I don't want to feel like I'm pressuring you."

Sabrina's entire body grew numb. How could she tell the man she loved, no? She drew in a deep breath, praying that she wouldn't regret this. It would be the first time she ever lied to him. "I'm all in," she said in the most comforting way she could muster. "I want this baby…and I want you." She didn't bat an eye as she fought back tears from the ignominy and degradation she would endure.

Luke lovingly stroked her thigh before stopping all at once to reach inside the bedside nightstand. He pulled out a pocket-size calendar. When she realized it was an ovulation chart, her eyes nearly crossed in disbelief. He pointed to the date, September 7th, which he had already circled in a bold red marker. The other highlighted dates were all too familiar. Unbeknownst to her, he had been tracking her menstrual and ovulation cycle. Stunned out of her mind and unable to express her thoughts with words, she stared intently at him as he flexed a crooked grin.

"It's show time!" he said lastly.

Serodiscordant relationship: *Also known as magnetic or mixed-status. One in which one partner is infected by HIV and the other is not.*

1

"How do you know, Greg?"

With sorrow—in her eyes, Nadine believed she had no other choice but to be honest with him. They had said they would leave their past in the past, but she knew that he needed to know.

"It's a long, long, story," she said.

"And I have all the time in the world to hear it."

With that, Nadine began to venture right back into the depths of her betrayal. A tumultuous past with a vengeance to destroy her present and her future. It was bitter. Angry. Yes, her past was even jealous and fearful of the threat of happiness, which only powered its engine to painstakingly contaminate every potential relationship, each opportunity it got.

Leonard deserved the truth. Her truth. And while perhaps a different day and milieu would have been more convenient for her, it was this unfortunate circumstance that led to her admission of knowing his best friend, Greg Adams—an arrogant son-of-a-bitch whom she detested. She had cursed the ground that his flat-footed, self-righteous ass walked on, and had hoped like hell she would never have to see his face again. Quite frankly, had Leonard not received that phone call an hour ago, informing him that Greg had shot himself in the head, she wouldn't be standing in this emergency room, coaxing her skeletons out of the closet.

She and Leonard were still getting to know each other on a

spiritual and emotional level, and because the relationship was so fresh, there was no way he was prepared to hear what she had yet to divulge. The burden alone of having to tell him, reminded her that she was a prisoner of her own secrets and a hostage of her own lies. It was depressing enough being in the very hospital her best friend, Denise, had died in. Now here they stood, waiting with baited breath for an update on Greg's condition. Her inaudible remorseful cry fell on deaf ears as time flitted by. She was hurting on the inside, but he couldn't have known it. No one could have.

She rubbed her hands up and down her arms. It was always so cold in hospitals. That much she remembered. But this day, the frigid temperature was mentally paralyzing. She wished she had thought to grab a sweater on their way out the door.

A short, plump, Hispanic woman passed by. She balanced a holder with four Starbucks cups in one hand, her gigantic purse, tote bag, and a red-and-blue fleece blanket in the other. The aromas mingled in the air, temporarily disguising the combination of various chemicals, melted plastic and body odor. It might have been all in her head, but every hospital she had ever been inside had this unique smell. It made her nauseous, not to mention it triggered her OCD to the point where she wanted to go on a hospital cleaning binge. Her eyes followed the woman. *I could use a cup of coffee right about now*, she thought. To warm her and to fully rouse her thoughts into perspective.

Leonard squared his shoulders, slightly raising his chin. The fold in his forehead, the unfamiliarity in his chocolate brown eyes, and the switch in his usually calm and laid-back demeanor, gave him away. She wanted to assure him it wasn't what he must have been thinking, but her tongue was cemented to the floor of her mouth, preventing her from relieving him of any man's worst fear. She would not have dared dreamed of sleeping with that jerk. Not in a million dreams or a million years. Not even if he was the last man on earth or even if they were stranded on an island. Her stomach did a double somersault to cosign her latest thought.

As grueling as it was, she had already accepted responsibility for her role in that twisted affair; now she had to figure out how to tell Leonard that she wasn't as perfect as her representative portrayed her to be. Certainly, she wasn't prepared to expose her flaws and unearth her secrets. The timing was bad. Extremely bad. But was there ever a *right* moment to admit your *wrong*doing? Most people usually swept their dirt under a rug, but there was no way she could do that. Not now. There was too much at risk. And better he hear it from her mouth than from his own best friend. But right now, was simply not the time or the place. They needed to be back there praying and consoling Greg's wife. Not standing here conferring about her dirty little secrets and bedroom drama. While Nadine quietly prayed that Greg would come out of this alive, she couldn't refrain from questioning if it was his own guilty conscience that coerced him to pull that trigger and blow the back of his brains out.

She wrestled with that thought. It seemed to remind her that every human being had to deal with their own demons in their own way. Who was she to judge Greg? Reflecting back on things now, they weren't so different. They were merely two imperfect people living in an imperfect world.

She inhaled a short unsteady breath as people continued to shuffle past them, headed in various directions. The words that slithered on the edge of her tongue, refused to make their exit and allow her the satisfaction of making this real quick and painless. Her eyes roved ardently, scanning every corner of the room for a quiet area to move their discussion.

"I was really hoping we could speak in private. From the looks of it…I don't think that's possible here. Are you sure you want to discuss this, now?" Her eyes pleaded with him to give her a pass.

She needed more time to figure out exactly how she was going to deliver everything. The boldness in his eyes held her captive.

"I think we're good here. Besides, I'm dying to hear this story."

The smile Nadine had grown quite fond of was absent. Her face tightened as the weight of her quandary sank deeply inside of her chest. Instantly, she came to grips with what she stood to lose. The possibility of a future with Leonard Dupree, seemed to dissolve before her very own eyes.

"I...uh..." she stammered, "really don't know where to begin." She bit down on her bottom lip as if that would transport every sweaty detail a lot faster. As if it would help her plead her case. She searched her mind high and low, being extremely cautious with her words, although there wasn't anything she could say to ease the blow or justify her actions.

"Baby, just talk to me." Leonard's face gleamed with concern and impatience, imploring her to spit it out, yet his tone was so gentle. Trusting. He made her feel safe. The exact same way she felt whenever he held her. Whenever he comforted her. Whenever he made sweet passionate love to her without even having to be inside of her body.

She stepped outside of herself, put her big-girl panties on and went for it. Only God knew where this would go.

"Leonard, I haven't been completely—" She stopped midsentence when her phone rang. Any other time she would have ignored Jeff's ringtone. His calls as of late had mostly been sexual proposals. Each time, Nadine had declined. Usually her rejections led them right back to square one. The past would come up; her so-called disloyalty to him would be thrown in her face, and then they would find themselves going back and forth about the same old things that didn't really matter anymore. However, today, she welcomed the interruption.

She whipped the phone out of her purse and pressed TALK before it could go to voicemail.

"Hello," she answered. She lifted a finger to Leonard, mouthing that it was Jeff. She plugged her left ear to drain out all the conversations happening around her.

"Where are you?" Jeff questioned.

"You have to speak up! I can barely hear you in here."

"I said where…are…you? We've been trying to…call…day…"

She had barely made out what he'd said. "Why? What's going on?" She listened more intently. Thought she heard sirens in the background but couldn't be for sure if it was coming from his end or hers. "Hello, Jeff!"

"Nadine, you're…breaking…up!"

"Jeff! Can you hear me?" Her phone pinged. She glanced at her screen to see that not only did her call just drop, but she only had two percent battery life.

"Is everything okay?" Leonard asked.

Her eyebrows furrowed as she looked up at him. "I don't know. The call dropped."

"Here, try mine." Leonard handed her his phone.

Nadine squeezed out a thank you, apprehension suddenly claiming her. Her fingers moved feverishly across the keypad. She walked a short distance away until she saw three bars light up. She stood frozen, praying she didn't lose the signal.

"Jeff Jackson," he answered on the first ring.

"It's me! What is going on?"

"What number are you calling me from?"

"That's irrelevant! Now what do you want, Jeff?"

"You need to get home. Now!"

"Why, what's happened?"

"There was a fire in your building! On your floor."

"Fire! Oh my God, Canvas!" Nadine panicked and became completely undone. Her breathing rapidly intensified. "My baby," she panted in uneven breaths. She balled her left hand into a fist and respired in and out of the opening.

"Calm down. He's with me."

"Oooh…thank God!" She exhaled, tears quickly filling her eyes. She placed her free hand over her heart. "I'm on my way," she said weakly as tears continued to flow from her beautiful brown eyes. She allowed the call to disconnect itself and rushed back over to Leonard. "I have to go!" Her words came out choppy but comprehensible.

Leonard reached for her trembling hands. "What's wrong?"

Fresh tears streamed down her unmade face. "There was a fire in my building," she sniffed.

"Dear God, Canvas!"

More tears clogged her throat. "He's okay. Jeff has him. But…I have to go." Her voice trailed off. "For all I know, I could be homeless right now."

Leonard nodded his understanding. "It's okay. And I'll be there as soon as I can."

Nadine nodded and tears dropped to her blouse. She couldn't think fast enough. Her mind was on her baby. "Are you going to be able to find a ride home?"

"Yes…yes…you go! I'll be fine."

She pressed her lips tightly together. "Okay." She handed him back his phone before turning on her heels and racing in the opposite direction.

"Drive safely!" Leonard hollered after her.

Nadine didn't look back. She needed to get to her baby. At that exact moment, seeing with her own two eyes that he was unharmed was the only thing that mattered.

2

J eff's heart nearly jumped out of his chest when he received the phone call a little less than an hour ago. His entire world came to a screeching halt, and the tight, wet space he was in, suddenly suffocated him.

He had been in the wrong place at the wrong time. Inside the wrong woman at the wrong time; that much, he had already kicked his own ass for. He knew damn well that he should not have gone there with *her*, of all people. So when he happened to glance over at his phone in the midst of carving his last name inside of her sweet apple cobbler and saw that it was lit with several missed calls and text message alerts from Casey, trepidation overtook him, allowing no other option but to submit and pull out, right at the cusp of his own sexual zenith.

The beautiful woman that had been conveniently situated underneath his long, hard body, was spent from sexual exhaustion and reaching an eternal euphoria that only Jeff Jackson could adeptly produce. Her silky golden-brown legs had been roped loosely around his neck while the spikey heels of her jade pumps, clinked in harmony. He had laid down the python as if it was her birthday; escorting her to a magical paradise that she would not soon forget. He had swum through the deepest end of her ocean, his name surfing and riding her gifted tongue, long and hard, putting shame to some of the best bull riders in the region. He was so confident in his abilities, his talents, his sex game, that he would be surprised if her neighbors hadn't already reported them for disturbing the peace.

Since he had promoted himself to an equal opportunity lover, he no longer placed limitations on himself. Hell, he was a single man, so he had a God-given right to exploit his manhood and celebrate his freedom. He had already missed an entire decade of his single life. Therefore, it was time to experiment. Black, White, Latino, Asian…it didn't matter; he loved the company and conversation of a fine-ass woman, but most importantly, he loved pussy. Therefore, it was only a matter of time before he rescued Sabrina from her misery and gave her what she had been surreptitiously begging for.

Nevertheless, after being intimate with Sabrina, despite their obvious attraction to one another since the beginning of the school year, only he was aware of the fact that today would be their first and last time together. Not because she wasn't what his dick yearned for during its time in need, but because she was indubitably a married woman. While he might have been burned from the flames of matrimonial Hell, he couldn't help but reserve some level of respect for the brothers who remained victims of it. His heart went out to each and every one of them, but more importantly, he didn't want no shit with her old man. She could keep that drama.

When word got out he was single again, women came out in droves, but married women were off-limits in his book. Sabrina's unhappiness wasn't any man's business, especially not his, unless of course she was venting to a male therapist. It was self-destructive. He should have known; he had used that information to his advantage. To make that connection. To earn her trust so that he could position himself for the biggest payoff—a lonesome pussy. The bragging rights of being able to say he knocked off his daughter's dance teacher had never crossed his mind. There had been numerous occasions during parent-teacher conferences where she took the time to open up to him. She had said she wanted a man's point of view, and today he had given her way more than his perspective. It was during the times she would invite herself over to wash or braid Deandra's hair, tutor her in math, or prepare them a week's worth of dinner that provided ample opportunity to get to know each other better. Like most men, he loved coddling a woman in distress, but this time, he had to shake off the pussy dust that prevented him from seeing things straight.

Jeff looked back at his son who was sleeping peacefully in his car seat. He inhaled deeply, thanking his Maker once again for allowing everyone to make it out of the building safely and in the nick of time. His attention returned to what used to be a row of luxury condominiums. The thick, black and gray smoke haze that blanketed Uptown Dallas had been visible for miles, way before he had arrived on the scene. It had taken firefighters nearly an hour to extinguish the blaze that had gutted Nadine's entire unit, leaving nothing but naked frames. His heart ached for her as he watched the authorities confer with the residents that shared Nadine's floor. The building was damaged beyond recognition and it was apparent that nothing could be salvaged. Nadine had lost everything. Everything she had worked so hard for had been reduced to ash.

He raised his head and caught a glimpse of Nadine's Audi in his rearview mirror, flying through the parking lot. She pulled alongside of him and hopped out before the car could come to a complete stop. She ran around to his side of the car and swung the back door open. Any more force would have ripped it clean off.

In his calmest of voices, "He's fine," Jeff assured her.

"My baby," Nadine murmured feebly. She cupped Canvas's face

and leaned in to kiss him. She placed her forehead against his and left it there for a moment.

"They got out just in time," Jeff said.

Nadine sniffed, unending tears pouring down her face. "Thank you, Jesus! Thank you, Lord! I would have died…if…something would have happened…to my baby!"

Jeff watched her through the rearview mirror. While he empathized with her in this moment, he still wanted to know where she had been and why in the hell she hadn't answered his and Casey's phone calls. If he had to take a guess, he would have bet a million bucks that she was with that flower guy, Mr. Try Too Hard. He sucked his teeth, aggravated at the thought of it. This was the same cat she had been taking his son around. If brotherman thought for one minute he was going to step in and play stepdaddy to Canvas Demond Jackson, he had another thing coming. Jeff was overprotective of both his children, and while their situation was extremely complicated, given that Canvas, his firstborn, was born from his mistress and not his wife, he loved Deandra and Canvas equally.

"Looks like that officer is heading over to speak to you." His little chat with her would have to wait for now. He adjusted the air conditioner and stepped out of the car. "How you doing there, Officer?"

"Perhaps I should be asking you fine folks that. It's unfortunate what's happened today. Good news is everybody got out safely."

They all nodded in agreement.

"How did the fire start?" Jeff inquired.

"Looks like someone had left their apartment with a candle unattended."

Jeff shook his head solemnly. "Gotta be more careful."

Nadine stood closely beside Jeff. "Oh my, God!" she shrieked, covering half her face as tears skated down her cheeks. "It was me. I left a candle lit. Oh my God!" she cried.

Jeff stared at her wide-eyed, but instead of scolding her like a child, he wrapped an arm around her. "It's okay," he said, hoping to soothe her pain.

"Were they able to recover anything?" Her sniffles were followed by a round of coughs.

The officer shook his head. "Unfortunately, ma'am, it's a total loss."

That triggered more tears. "All of my pictures…my memories…" She coughed more.

"You okay?" Jeff and the officer asked simultaneously.

Nadine started wheezing. She grabbed her chest, trying to breathe.

"It's the smoke! She's having an asthma attack!" Jeff exclaimed.

The officer's eyes bucked and he rushed off to get help.

Jeff looped Nadine's arm around his neck and clamped his left arm around her waist to prevent her from passing out. "Where's your inhaler?"

Nadine gasped for air. She managed to point in the direction of the charred building.

"Look at me," he said. "Breathe. Slow. Breathe." He held her tightly and tried his best to keep her calm. Her shoulders eventually began to relax and her hands stopped trembling. "It's okay. I got you."

The officer returned with one of the paramedics who quickly helped Jeff ease her onto the stretcher. An oxygen mask was immediately placed over Nadine's face to stabilize her breathing.

"You're going to be just fine," Jeff assured her. He gently rubbed her hands. Before he could reestablish that overdue connection, his Bluetooth went off. He hit the button without checking his phone to see who the call was coming from. "Jeff Jackson."

"How you doing? This is Leonard. Does Nadine happen to be around?"

Jeff glanced down at Nadine with an indiscernible disdain. "Sorry, my man. She's a little tied up right now. Or shall I say, *we're* tied up. Better luck next time."

Click.

3

Better luck next time?

Leonard allowed Jeff's words to punch him smack in the face. He knew when he was being tested, and Jeff—Nadine's sperm donor, as she had referred to him on countless occasions—was obviously testing him.

Before he could slide in a cool collected response, Jeff had terminated the call. Leonard managed a quiet chuckle as he pulled the phone from his ear and smoothly clipped it back on his hip. Jeff's insolence had challenged his better judgment, but he refused to regale superfluous foolishness. Another man's insecurities were not his problem. It was obvious the brotha's bitterness stemmed from having his heart split in half, but Leonard could not have cared less.

There were still so many questions swarming around in his head that he could barely concentrate on the matter at hand. He turned the corner and picked up his pace, passing a sea of individuals waiting to be processed or called to the back to be seen by a doctor. This environment was a threat to his health, but he needed to be here for Vivian and Greg; to see to it that he pulled through this.

Vivian's sapphire-blue eyes landed on his the second he entered the waiting room. Her arms were crossed comfortably over her bosom and one leg straddled the other as her troubled gaze slipped away from him. The light above skittered over her. Her wispy blonde hair was tucked behind her ears, revealing every subtle feature of her face. Even in distress, she was admirable. He only wished there was something more he could do to ease her pain.

He claimed a seat beside her.

"Any word?"

She shook her head solemnly. Lips pressed tight, she closed her eyes and reopened them.

"I don't know what he was thinking," she said. "What could have been so bad between us to force him to resort to this, huh?" Her tears seemed to melt her makeup as the black streaks from her mascara stained her ivory skin. "I had forgiven him," she muttered.

Leonard listened intently.

"I'm sure you're aware that my husband was unfaithful to me. As painful as it is…I forgave him." She sniffled. "So for him to resort to such a cowardly act…to abandon me, again…is unfair. He *cannot* leave me this way! He can't." Her voice cracked and everything thereafter was indiscernible.

Leonard placed an arm around her shoulder. "It's okay, Vivian. He's going to pull through this. We have to remain in faith."

Vivian unleashed another soft wail, grabbing the attention of everyone in the room.

"I would do anything for my husband. I love him so much, Leonard. I would die if anything happens to him," she cried.

His chest tightened as her words echoed in his mind. Greg had been wrong about Vivian. Damn wrong. This woman loved him. Leonard's conscience ate at him, but hearing Vivian pour out her heart for her husband, reassured him in a way that granted him instant relief. It was confirmation that he had done the right thing by not filing the divorce papers when Greg had instructed him to. He had only been looking out for his friend, and if he had not followed his first mind, Greg would have made one of the biggest mistakes of his life.

Time heals all wounds, his mother would always say. And that's exactly what he believed would repair Greg and Vivian's marriage. He was sure of it.

Vivian nestled her head against his chest. Her breathing grew heavier.

"God, please. Please see my husband through this," she kept saying as she held her hands in a prayer fold.

An aging black woman, who had been seated near the entrance, struggled to her feet. She scooted her walker across the floor in their direction. She stopped directly in front of them, then reached into the small purse strapped across her chest.

Leonard smiled at the woman as she pulled out a travel-size pack of Kleenex. She retrieved a single sheet from the pack and extended her hand toward Vivian.

"Ever thang gonna be all right, chile. God is in *full* control of your situation!"

"Thank you, ma'am." Vivian blotted her eyes with the tissue.

The woman turned slowly on her heels. The hem of her long, full, floral skirt swept the floor as she pushed the walker back to the other side.

Leonard allowed his head to fall against the wall. Nadine intercepted his thoughts again. He couldn't move past it. How did she know Greg? He wondered if they had ever dated, and if so, if Greg had ever mentioned having an HIV-positive friend—as if that should even come up; but it very well could have. It had happened before. His own sister, Keisha, had once told a girlfriend of hers who he had considered asking out on a date, all of his personal business. If she had done it to him, who was to say that Greg wasn't capable of being reckless with his mouth too. It was true that everyone had secrets and a past, but not the kind of secret Leonard had. All of his past relationships had been failures because of it. They couldn't envision a future with a man who was living with HIV. Couldn't get past his condition and love him for who he was. Instead, they quickly and quietly removed themselves from his life. It was why he hadn't told Nadine yet. He was afraid she would do what the others had done. But this time around, he wouldn't be so naïve. He needed to protect his own heart from being trampled over. Regardless of if they showed it, men had feelings too. He reasoned that if Nadine was the right one for him; loving, compassionate, genuine and understanding, he would know in due time. And only then would he share this secret he'd been harboring.

Vivian slowly lifted her blonde head, shaking him out of his thoughts. She leaned back fully in her own chair, her eyes dazedly scanning the overcrowded room. Her sniffles grew fainter as the minutes passed. This waiting was killing him. He reached for his cell to check the time and saw that he had a missed text message from his baby sister, Tracey. She wanted to know if he had made up his mind about attending Thanksgiving at her house. He held a mental debate. After everything that had transpired last year, he wasn't sure if he was ready to make that trip back to East Texas to be forced to face his big-mouthed sister, Keisha, who had embarrassed the hell out of him. As always, she would be there, and another confrontational family reunion was not something he was looking forward to.

"Where did your girlfriend ease off to?" Vivian uttered quietly.

Leonard cleared his throat. "She umm…had an emergency. Received a call not too long ago that her apartment building had caught on fire."

Her mouth fell agape. "Oh goodness. It's one horrible thing after another." She shook her head. "If there's anything I can do to help, please let me know."

"Thank you."

She stared into thin air. "Seems as though the poor girl has an affinity for trouble."

Leonard's eyebrows met as confusion washed over his face. "How do you mean?"

She turned back to him, an uneven smile gripping her lips.

"Nadine, is it?"

Leonard nodded slowly, his curiosity piqued even further now.

"Greg and I had pulled her out of a limbo a short while back. Poor girl's tire had given out on her."

"Oh…I see." He nodded slowly as that puzzle piece landed right in his lap. Why didn't Nadine come right out and say that? He had been worried all for nothing.

"Mrs. Adams," a slender black woman in hospital scrubs announced. Her eyes searched the sea of faces in the room.

Leonard and Vivian both stood to their feet, making immediate eye contact with her.

"Follow me, please," the nurse aide smiled.

Vivian walked ahead and Leonard followed closely behind as the aide led them down the corridor, inside an elevator, and through another area of the hospital. When they reached the Intensive Care Unit, she slid back the third curtain where they'd arrived.

"Please have a seat." She gestured toward the two empty chairs. "Dr. Gordy will be in shortly to speak with both of you."

Before the woman could simply neglect their worries, "Can you at least tell us if he's alive or not?" Vivian questioned.

The aide lent a sympathetic look. "Since I don't have the latest update on the patient, I'm unable to provide any information. I do apologize, but Dr. Gordy will be here to answer all of your questions."

Vivian's brooding eyes tore away from the woman. Her hands seemed to resist the calm she tried to force upon them as she managed a seat in one of the hard blue chairs. She sighed loudly, crossed her arms over her bosom and mumbled something Leonard could not quite interpret.

"We'll be here," Leonard told the aide. She offered a smile, her eyes apologizing for the inconvenience. He drew in a deep breath and took a seat in the second chair. He said a silent prayer, hoping that the news to come would be positive.

Minutes turned into a full hour later, and they had yet to hear from Dr. Gordy. No one had come back to give them a report on Greg's condition. "I'm going to go find out what's going on. This is flat-out ridiculous!" Leonard hopped up from that uncomfortable chair. His stern, wrinkled face was transparent to his displeasure.

"Please see to it, Leonard. My patience has worn thin."

As Leonard snatched back the cream-colored curtain to track down someone who could update him, Dr. Gordy stood in front of him, peering down at the chart in his hand. The doctor immediately looked up, apparently startled.

"Adams family?" the doctor questioned.

"Yes!" Leonard and Vivian replied in unison and angst.

The doctor stepped farther inside the small space. Vivian rose to her feet. She fingered her wedding ring, extreme worry masked behind her oceanic-blue eyes. Leonard's heart pounded within his chest, and his bald head began to sweat under the direct lighting pouring from the ceiling. His worry and fear of hearing anything other than that his best friend was alive, got the best of him, and the doctor's delay in delivering the news wasn't helping any.

"Please tell us you have good news," Vivian said. Her left hand covered her heart.

Dr. Gordy dropped his hands to his side and looked them square in the eyes. "Mr. Adams is in *critical*, but stable condition. He's in the intensive care unit until his vitals improve."

"Thank God!" Leonard exclaimed, exhaling. This was the news he'd waited for all evening.

Vivian held her silence. She folded her hands and placed them over her quivering mouth. "He's alive," she uttered robotically, staring raptly at Dr. Gordy.

"Yes, he's going to survive," the doctor confirmed. "He's lucky to have been rushed here in time. A minute later and we would have lost him."

Leonard couldn't imagine losing his only true friend. The doctor's words echoed in his mind as he tried to process everything.

"We were able to extract the bullet from his brain successfully, however, there's still a great deal of swelling." Dr. Gordy went into detail, explaining how the trajectory of the bullet had caused some damage. The extent of the damage had yet to be determined due to the amount of swelling.

"Is he alert?" Vivian questioned.

"No. He's currently sedated. We'll keep him in a medically induced coma until the swelling subsides. This way he's comfortable."

"And exactly how long will that be?" Vivian pressed further. "How long before he's talking?" she asked more precisely.

"It's difficult to gauge accurately. It could be days, weeks...or perhaps months."

Leonard gasped. "Months!"

Dr. Gordy nodded. "I must also make you aware that it's quite likely Mr. Adams won't recall what happened to him."

"You mean he won't remember shooting himself?" Vivian interjected.

"Correct. We refer to it as post-traumatic amnesia. It's a mental state in which the survivor becomes disoriented and is unable to connect continuous memories, or events. With brain injuries such as his, there's a strong possibility Mr. Adams' memory may lapse, or erase altogether."

Leonard's heart sunk as the doctor predicted Greg's fate. "Amnesia?" he muttered, shaking his head jadedly. This was a hard pill to swallow. "There's gotta be something you can do to prevent that from happening, Doc."

"I can assure you we're doing everything we can. At this point, all we can do is wait for him to come around."

There was an eerie silence that floated over them. Leonard was hiding behind his emotions, trying his best to keep it together for Vivian's sake. He eyed Dr. Gordy gravely whose sleep-deprived eyes hauled bags the size of walnuts. It was apparent he had his fair share of sleepless nights. Instantly, Leonard's respect for the doctor became paramount. Leonard rubbed Vivian's back as she blotted her teary eyes. This was hard on the both of them. Greg was a good dude. A pompous and egotistical bastard the majority of the time, but nonetheless, a good dude. From the time he received the call, Leonard replayed every last one of their conversations. None of this added up. Greg had major problems, but he never gave Leonard a reason to believe that he was suicidal. Not one reason. Leonard could only speculate that perhaps it was Greg's extramarital affairs that had gotten the best of him, but what he couldn't understand was why Greg would go this far after he had carefully prepared himself mentally and financially for the divorce he was secretly filing behind Vivian's back. Things didn't appear so damnable until now.

"Did you have any more questions for me?"

Leonard glanced back over at Vivian, her angelic alabaster face flustered. She appeared spaced out and in her own little world. Everything was raining down on them way too fast. He couldn't erase the mental image he conjured of Greg putting that gun to his own damn head. Perhaps Vivian was experiencing the same voltage of shock as he.

"When can I see my husband?" Vivian asked monotonously.

Dr. Gordy fared a stiff, yet seemingly genuine smile. "I'll be more than happy to walk you both back now."

4

"Thanks for the lift," Naomi said. "My husband normally drives the way when we're here." She chuckled lightly. "I'm actually embarrassed to admit that my sense of direction is terrible without him," she told her new fabulous and famous friend, Ebony, whom she had met only hours earlier. They had chatted the entire flight from Dallas to Los Angeles like old girlfriends.

"No sweat! I'm always willing to help someone in need. That's what I do. Besides, you wouldn't have gotten very far without a cell phone or a GPS, honey. That's a necessity, you know."

Naomi didn't have a phone as she had given it back to Maribel. It had been her only lifeline. Her only connection to Greg during the duration of the assignment.

"Yeah, I imagine it's pretty easy to get lost in a big city such as this one," she said. She climbed out of the car and went to the trunk to retrieve her luggage. Good thing she only had two suitcases. The trips her and Greg had made back and forth in an effort to make the transition smooth and discreet, had proven to be beneficial. The majority of her things from the condo were already in the new house.

"Well, if you're ever in the area, don't hesitate to drop by. We can do lunch or something."

"That sounds divine!"

Naomi absolutely loved Ebony's accent. She had said she was

originally from Detroit but had inherited the dialect while living in London for a stint. The young actress reeked superstardom and Naomi was lucky to have met a rising star. She was even impressed with Ebony's style—full of pizzazz that Naomi wished she possessed. Listening to Ebony talk about herself on the plane and entire car ride home, had made Naomi wish she had half the energy and confidence Ebony consumed. Had that been the case, she would have hopped back on that plane to go get her man.

Ebony removed the designer shades from her face. "I wasn't going to say anything, but in the next couple of weeks, I'll be shooting a love scene with Denzel Washington." She exposed her pearly whites. Her flawless skin had been kissed by the morning sun. "I may be able to pull some strings and get you a pass to come on set."

Naomi's eyes grew big as saucers. She loved her some Denzel. Seen every single movie he had played in from the 1984 *A Soldier's Story* to his latest. She was not as much as a movie geek as her ex-husband, Charles, but anything that featured the one and only Denzel Washington was worthy of her support.

"Let me make sure I heard you correctly. Did you say, Denzel Washington?"

Ebony nodded. A Cheshire grin planted across her face. "I would *love* to meet him! I'm a huge fan of his work."

"I'm sure I can arrange that. My producer knows everyone in Hollywood," Ebony bragged.

Naomi's face lit up like a teenager's. "Wow. I look forward to it. Thank you! I'll call you tomorrow and give you my new number the second I get a phone. It's likely I won't stray very far from home since I'm still adapting to the city."

"Sistah, please! This is L.A. La-la Land of illusions. You better live it up, honey. Do some sightseeing. I know I sure as hell plan to." Ebony smacked her lips. "You can be *whoever* you want to be here and do whatever your heart desires." She smiled wickedly.

"No one would ever know." She winked her eye. "Stay fierce, doll! I have to skedaddle. Don't want to keep the producers waiting." She waved goodbye and slowly pulled away from the curb.

Naomi stood there for a second longer to take in the beautiful scenery. Immaculate multimillion-dollar homes lined both sides of her street along with fine luxurious vehicles that exhibited wealth and good living. This was all surreal. It seemed like it was only yesterday that she was nursing her alcohol addiction, living on the streets, and selling her body for money and shelter, or whichever was available. Now, she was healthy, rich, and living like royalty. If only her ex-husband and kids could see her now.

Keys in hand, she started for the $5 million mansion she had fallen in love with the second she laid eyes on it. She stopped midstep when her neighbor's Yorkie came charging toward her across the freshly cut grass. The dog danced at her feet, wagging its tail. She set her things down and scooped the friendly animal up, rubbing its head.

"Hello to you too," she said.

"Sunshine!" the Asian woman called after the dog. "Sunshine, stop bothering this lady!" She walked quickly over to Naomi, who met her halfway. "I'm so very sorry. She always gets excited whenever I let her off the leash."

Naomi handed the well-groomed dog over. "Don't worry. I love animals." She smiled. "Besides, Sunshine's a cutie pie. She's welcomed over anytime."

"Thank you." A loose grin jerked at the woman's thin lips. "I'm Yah Ming. You can call me Ming, for short." She extended her hand.

"Pleased to meet you." Naomi smiled as she thought about what Ebony had said. She was right. It was time she lived a little. L.A. was going to give her the opportunity to start over with her life. Completely over. "Ming, I'm Denise…Denise Adams. Your new neighbor."

5

"What the hell am I doing here?" Nadine questioned incredulously. She hadn't meant to sound so churlish, but she wasn't in the best of moods right now. "This was a bad idea. I can't stay here and you know it."

Jeff shut off the water after rinsing out one of Canvas's Sippy cups. He walked back into the living room area, a few feet shy of where she sat, closed-legged, stiff, and out of sorts. Their eyes met briefly. Long enough for her to recall how shitty he'd acted this morning when they spoke, and quick enough for her to realize that *her* problems were *her* problems alone. Her refusal to grant him the satisfaction of watching her suffer in her state of destitution had been pride driven. She hadn't enlisted his charity and in no way was she suddenly desperate for his time and attention. Nadine sponsored her own pity-parties. She didn't need a man to run to her rescue. It was Jeff who had taught her that. Taught her that if a man tore his ass and left you cradling your pillow and crying your eyes out every night, the same inner strength you used to bounce back after that heartbreak, was the same inner strength you used to get through tough shit like this.

She had already been dealing with enough lately, and losing everything in the fire was the tip of the iceberg. Every single thing she had busted her ass for had gone up in flames, leaving her and Canvas homeless and with nothing but the clothes on their back and the shoes on their feet.

She picked up her phone and began scrolling through all the missed calls and text messages. She had only informed Belinda, her receptionist, who in turn sent out the memo to every last one of her staff members at Platinum Crest Investments. They had all called or sent texts to express their deepest sympathies. A few of them had even offered her money and a place to stay, aware that Nadine didn't have any family in Texas. Jeff had been the closest thing to it. That's if sperm donors counted as family. Besides Jeff, she and Canvas were pretty much on their own.

Reading all the texts quickly reduced her to tears. It made things painfully clear. This was actually happening to her, and she almost couldn't believe it. Couldn't believe God was still punishing her for what she had done. She blotted her eyes with her knuckles. She wanted so badly to scream and let it all out, but she refused to be this vulnerable in front of him.

Jeff handed the juice-filled cup to Canvas along with an animal cracker. They watched him waddle back toward Deandra's room.

"He's on his way back, Deandra!"

"Okay. I got him, Daddy!" Deandra hollered back.

Nadine's eyes curiously roamed the living room. To her surprise, the place was spotless. It appeared having a new woman in his life might have actually done Jeff some good. Pictures of her departed friend evoked painful memories. She hadn't stepped a foot in that house since Denise died. Not one foot. And when it was all said and done, of all the places in the world she could have gone, this was the *last* place she needed to be. There was no way in hell she should have been sitting here on Denise's favorite couch, in her space, drowning in her own misery and feeling sorry for herself. She had lost that privilege years ago.

She broke her troubled gaze and it landed on Jeff's feet. He had gotten comfortable on the other sofa. Too comfortable. He reached for the remote and powered on the television, parking it on Animal Planet of all things. While he quickly absorbed himself in the program, a glimpse of what their life once was collided with where she stood with Leonard. She couldn't negate her true feelings for Jeff as much as she wanted to. It wasn't that simple. The heart always disobeyed the mind, and here again, that seemed to be the case.

She found it difficult being in his presence, especially after he had showed her how expendable she was to him. To get engaged to another woman after promising to marry her, left an angry and bitter taste in her mouth. Maybe that was more of the reason why she knew she shouldn't be here expecting…needing…wanting… something she would never get—closure. Yet the thought of him making himself wholly available to watch after her, almost renewed her trust in him. She couldn't readily recall a time when he'd ever been so altruistic. Maybe he still cared. She allowed that possibility to linger in her mind. It almost made her want to forget about how bad it hurt. Almost.

Jeff arrested her attention again.

"Are you okay now?"

"Is that supposed to be a trick question?" she snarled.

"Baby…"

Nadine shifted uncomfortably.

"I mean…Nadine. I know you have a lot on your mind right now. But I'm here for you. We're in this together."

"Humph! Together?" A smile cracked her lips open, exposing her pearly whites.

"Yes…*together.*"

She looked around the elaborate lofty living room of his huge house before returning her attention to him. "There's only one of us homeless right now. And that's me," she scoffed.

"You're *not* homeless, so stop saying that. You can stay right here for as long as you'd like. There's plenty of room."

She shook her head. He wasn't getting it and probably never will. "Thank you, but no thank you," she said simply.

His face was immediately transfixed with confusion. He leaned forward, scrutinizing her. With his lip upturned, "You hate me that much that you can't even accept my helping hand?" he asked dubiously.

Recognizing the road this conversation was headed, she came to her feet. "Hate is such a strong word. Besides, your *fiancée* may not like the idea of me moving in," she abrasively pointed out. She shuffled past him, headed straight for Deandra's room. Her tongue was on fire, and it took everything in her not to say what was really on her mind. "Canvas!"

"Nadine!" Jeff called after her. "I've been meaning to talk to you about that."

Nadine allowed his calls to fall on deaf ears. She may have been a fool once, but she refused to be a fool twice by falling for any more of his bullshit.

She opened Deandra's bedroom door to find her practicing her dance moves. When she turned around and saw Nadine, she snatched off her pink headphones.

"Ugh! Can you learn how to knock?" Deandra's menacing eyes rolled so hard, any harder and they would have popped out and rolled right across the floor.

"Deandra, that's no way to speak to an adult. What's gotten into you, little girl?"

Deandra rolled her eyes again and held her hand in a stopping gesture. "Whatever! You're not my mama and you sho' not my daddy's girlfriend," she quipped, flipping her Senegalese twists across her shoulders. She secured the earphones back over her ears and jumped right back into her routine. She started up again as if Nadine were invisible.

Nadine's eyes narrowed to slits as she looked her goddaughter upside her head. It took everything in her not to walk over to Deandra and slap the spit out of her ten-year-old mouth. She commenced to scoop up her son before she did or said something that might invite the unwanted attention of Child Protective Services. She walked quickly through the house and back into the den to collect her purse.

Visibly confounded, "Where are you going?" Jeff probed. He shot up from the sofa.

"To a hotel."

"Hotel!"

"Your hearing seems to be perfectly fine," she remarked, a hint of sarcasm laced in her tone.

She grabbed Canvas's diaper bag and slung it over her right shoulder.

"At least leave Canvas here. I don't want my son cooped up in some sooty hotel room some old man's been fucking in all day, when he has his own room and bed right here."

"Don't share all your secrets."

"What the hell is that supposed to mean? You know what...I don't even wanna know."

After what happened earlier today, she was not going to let Canvas out of her sight, and it was unfortunate if Jeff couldn't understand that. "He's coming with me," she replied calmly. "I'll call you when we settle into the room. Consider it a courtesy for all you've done today." With Canvas on her hip, she walked around the coffee table, headed for the door.

Jeff exhaled sharply. "You're impossible. All I'm trying to do is help and you're pushing me away. That's always been your problem."

That got her attention. "Exactly what the hell are you saying?"

Jeff stopped, seemingly sorting his words. "Forget it. Humph…"

She could sense there was more he wanted to say, but his eyes began to stray.

"Call me when you make it to the room."

"No! What do you mean that's always been my problem? You said it, own it!"

"Let it go, Nadine." He shook his head back and forth. "It's not the time. You've been through enough today," he affirmed.

She stared at him long enough to realize that she needed to preserve her energy. She would need it tomorrow when she contacted the insurance company, the bank, and the realtor. She started for the door again with a little more pep in her step. She pulled it open and before she could gather any words, the woman before her spoke first. She was apparently caught off guard as much as Nadine was. The woman smiled tenderly at Nadine and her son. Nadine assessed the woman, all while suspecting her to be Jeff's fiancée. "Good evening," she replied pragmatically. The woman's hazel-green eyes fell to a soft squint, and her contagious smile forced Nadine to relinquish.

"Nadine, right?"

Nadine gave her an unsure nod, completely caught off guard by the woman's extra-friendly approach.

"It's nice to *finally* meet you. Jeff talks about you all the time. I feel like I already know you."

Nadine's eyes nearly crossed. She looked back at Jeff and a spurious grin played on his lips. "Well, that's nice to know." She cleared her throat. "I'm sorry…I didn't catch your name." She readjusted Canvas who had caused her entire arm to go numb.

"Pardon my manners. I'm Sabrina Montgomery! Deandra's dance teacher."

Since when did dance teachers start making late-night house calls? Nadine thought. "Sabrina. Okay." Nadine cut her eyes back at Jeff and smiled halfheartedly. "Well…it was nice meeting you. I guess I'll get on out of your way." Sabrina graciously stepped to the side, her perfect smile seemingly painted on her face. Nadine excused herself and made a beeline to the car.

"Call me as soon as you guys get settled in," Jeff called out to her.

Nadine hurriedly strapped Canvas in the car seat before climbing in front. She had to get as far away from there as she could. Jeff didn't deserve to witness the stream of recycled tears pouring down the rosy apples of her cheeks. She would not give him the pleasure in knowing that deep down, behind the mask, was a woman who had not only been burned by the fire but whose heart was heavy with regret.

6

S abrina slipped past him, her left hand slightly grazing his
crotch. Had he not known any better, he would have thought
she was feeling him up to see if his dick was harder than it
had been earlier that day. And it was. Especially after being around
Nadine for this long.

Jeff eased the door shut. Locked it. His impure thoughts with
his baby mama and the fact that she was still stuck on that twisted
lie Ménage had bottle-fed Deandra about them getting married
and making Nadine a maid. It was a joke that had gone too damn far.
A joke that should have never been played. That scandalous broad
had corrupted his daughter right under his own damn nose and
roof. He had been hoodwinked by a prostitute—the bottom feeder
of all the promiscuous societal thots in the U.S.A. His homies had
laughed at him. Told him he should have seen it coming and
smelled her scheming ass a mile away, especially after that nine-
year scandal his own wife had calculated. But Jeff didn't see it coming,
and now he had to bounce back from it once again. Every woman
he allowed to enter his life had scandalized him—Denise, Nadine,
and Ménage. It made him look at women as though they all came
packaged with hidden agendas. All of them.

Sabrina skirted past him dressed in a jade chiffon blouse that
accentuated her neckline, snow-white trousers, and matching multi-
colored jade, silver and white jeweled pumps. She made herself
right at home, as she did on every unexpected visit.

"So I finally got to meet the *infamous* Nadine," she said snidely.

Jeff met her sinister grin. "Humph! You know damn well you weren't trying to bump into my baby mama like that," he retorted with a light chuckle.

"You know me so well." She smiled. "I guess I'll admit that it was a little awkward."

He nodded in agreement, pulling in his bottom lip as he gave her a full once-over. "Only a little?"

She smiled. "Ooookay…it was pretty damn uncomfortable." She laughed.

Jeff released a short, guttural laugh. "Ugh-huh. That's what I thought."

They both got quiet.

"I would have probably felt the same way had I bumped into your old man."

Sabrina's eyes met his again. "Well, that will never happen."

"Can't be too sure. Did you forget that you only live two streets over?"

Sabrina smiled, angling her head slightly. "And what would you do if you did happen to encounter Mr. Montgomery?"

Jeff didn't miss a beat in responding, but he knew the question was a flat-out setup to see how jealous he was. "I wouldn't do a damn thing," he quipped in the most nonchalant manner.

Sabrina pursed her lips. "Nothing?" she questioned flatly. Her green eyes seemed to flicker with every word that coursed from her beautiful curvy lips.

Jeff shook his head and gave her a stern look. "Your husband is not any of my business."

"But you are fucking his wife." She smiled sexily, tempting him in more ways than one.

Jeff rested on her last remark as she switched in the direction of the kitchen. Although he didn't know what the brother looked like, he had no intentions on finding out. Again, it was none of his damn business. The less he knew, the better off he was.

Sabrina returned with two ice-cold beers. Her exotic features weakened him in the worst way. From the curve of her lips to the winding of her hips, which seemed to make music with every step that she took, Jeff wanted her again. As much as he tried, he could not quiet his lustful thoughts. He had already seen her naked. Had already toured her estate and placed his bid. He knew the pussy inside and out so there was no need to pretend that they were only friends. In a split-second they had become much more than that.

"Care to join me?" she asked.

"Thanks. I could use one of these right about now." Jeff quickly twisted the cap off and took a healthy swig. He followed her over to the bar and pulled out a chair for her and then a chair for himself. He had a lot on his mind, but he wasn't going to burden Sabrina with it. She had her own problems to deal with. "So what you doing creeping after dark?"

Sabrina took a sip of her beer. "I thought I'd come check on you. You rushed off earlier and left me hanging all by my lonesome. Just when it was getting soooo good."

Her long, silky hair was pulled back into a sleek ponytail that hung slightly past her shoulder. Her muted makeup amplified her smooth peach skin, flattering her natural beauty and making it damn near impossible to resist the sexual enticement. Their chemistry was deep and once before, they had gone as far as admitting to one another that late at night, they fantasized and longed for each other's touch. Although for Jeff, it was merely a convenient pillow confession. He dreamt about all the women he was sexually attracted to so Sabrina wasn't special in that regard.

Now as he stared at her, he felt profoundly sorry for her. Sorry that she had given herself to him out of hurt, resentment, and reprisal for her husband. Jeff had willingly allowed her to use him however she saw fit, but he knew she would not see it that way. She would blame him for her actions once he acknowledged that this wasn't going anywhere. Once he admitted that he wasn't looking for commitment, a relationship, or marriage. All he wanted was to Cadillac and catch up on lost time.

"Penny for your thoughts." Sabrina arched her left eyebrow, seemingly surprised that he was short on conversation tonight. She placed the brew on a wooden coaster and crossed a leg over the other. The gesture aroused him. He had witnessed with his own two eyes what those flexible legs of hers could do in the most compromising position.

He cleared his throat and rechanneled his thoughts. "Just thinking."

"About?"

He shook his head. "Nothing too important." He met her curiosity. He assessed her once more for the hell of it.

"Do you still love her?" Sabrina asked out of nowhere.

His face scrunched all on its own as he stared her in the eyes. "Where did that come from?"

"Jeff, answer the question," she said softly.

He finished off the beer and tried to avert his gaze. With her delicate touch, Sabrina cupped his chin between her fingers. "Stop pussyfooting with me. Are you still in love with Nadine?"

Staring into her hypnotic eyes, he fought back the only answer that would set him free, and instead, leaned in to kiss her. To quiet her worries. To lessen the blow that would surely come in due time. He stood from the chair and slowly unbuttoned her blouse, parting it right down the middle. To his advantage, she wasn't wearing a bra and if he was lucky, she wasn't wearing any panties either. His hands moved fanatically over the mountains of her jutting breasts, which appeared even more eager than Jeff to experience each other all over again. He sprinkled his DNA in sweet and tender strokes across her neck, careful to not leave his trademark of passion. He was considerate when he wanted to be. He began to drag his tongue and wrap his lips around her decadent chocolate ornaments, plucking them with his teeth before nestling them once again with his long warm tongue.

"Oh yes," Sabrina moaned softly in his ear. She wrapped her lean legs tightly around his waist, pulling him closer to her body.

Afraid Deandra would walk in, he hoisted her off the bar stool and carried her into his bedroom. He laid her across the bed, and they quickly shed every article of clothing they wore. He grabbed her by the ankles and pulled her all the way to the edge of the bed. He wanted her so bad, beads of sweat permeated his forehead. His tongue swept over her swollen, dripping pussy before diving deeply inside. To no surprise, she readily received him, cumming on his tongue before he could make second base. Before he could counter how this episode would play out, Sabrina had taken full control of the situation. She peeled back the sheets and pulled him into the middle of the bed. She rolled her lips expertly down his rod in an easy manner. Unable to take him all in, she folded her lips around him like a taco, drenching him with her heated saliva. His toes curled from the surge of electricity shooting through his entire body. His eyes drifted shut, and Nadine's beautiful face became the center of his concentration. By his own admission, her amber-brown eyes and delicious smooth butterscotch skin was the object of his affections. He imagined that it was *her* lips gripping his rock-hard flesh; her warm, wet pussy riding his cargo; and her long, sexy legs wrapped around his back.

As his mind escaped him, Sabrina ostensibly entrusted her womanly wiles to seduce, manipulate, and convince his dick that she was the *only* woman in his life. But unfortunately, the verdict was still out. As feeble as they both were in the heat of their intimacy, they refused to come down from that liquid ecstasy of a high. Jeff's only hope was that she would accept her wakeup call in the morning. The call that would slowly reintroduce them to their realities, supplying sufficient evidence to support their own versions of the truth. She was an unhappily married woman searching for love and affection, and Jeff was simply relishing the free ride.

7

"It's okay, Mommy's got the baby," Nadine sang to her crying son. She inserted the keycard into the door and pushed it open when the green light flashed. Canvas in one hand, she swept the wall for the light switch. When she found it, she hurried over to the couch, set her things down and comforted him. She rocked him gently in her arms, believing that he could sense their crisis. They were homeless. Homeless. The more she thought about their state of being, the more tears flooded her face. She inhaled deeply and slowly released the air. She had always been careful about not leaving candles unattended and knowing that she had in fact caused the fire was devastating. It was all her fault that many of the residents in her building were now without a place to stay. She could never forgive herself for this.

After Canvas was finally calm, Nadine fed him, bathed him, and put him down for bed. She was mentally and physically drained but there was nothing she could do to relax. She turned on the television, but seeing her charred building on the nine o'clock news only made this feel more real. For once, she had wished this was another one of her awful nightmares.

Parking the channel on BET, she thought again about all the phone calls she would need to make first thing Monday morning. She had to also factor in the daunting process of finding somewhere to live. After having Canvas, she had strongly considered finding a bigger place and starting anew, but she sure as hell hadn't planned on it happening this soon and under these circumstances. *When it rains, it pours*, she thought, staring vacantly into space.

She reached for the small notepad and shiny silver pen on the desk, complimentary of the Ritz. She began jotting down a general list of items that she'd lost in the fire. She didn't get very far before her tears began to smear the blue ink. It was pointless to do this right now. Calling her Aunt Mickey and informing her of what had happened crossed her mind, but after checking the time, she decided against it. Atlanta was an hour earlier in time difference, and knowing her Aunt Mickey, she was sound asleep at this hour. She got up from the bed and walked over to the table where her phone had been charging. She powered it back on. As she figured, there were several missed calls and texts. Sadly enough, she was not in the mood to talk to anyone except him. Seeing his face light up her screen the instant she tapped his number made her warm inside. It was as if he was there in the room with her, holding her, comforting her. The phone rang once and it felt like an eternity.

"Are you all right?" was the first thing out of his mouth. His soothing voice and tender touch always managed to kiss her soul.

"Can't truly say that I am," she replied. "But I'll get through this."

"Where are you?"

"A hotel."

"Hotel?"

"Yes."

Silence.

"Which hotel?"

"The Ritz-Carlton. On McKinney."

"I'm on my way."

"What do you mean?"

"You're coming to my place. I have plenty of space. You and Canvas can stay as long as you'd like."

"I don't want to be a burden, Leonard. You're dealing with enough right now with your friend. I'm…"

"Nadine," he interrupted. "Everything's going to be okay," he reassured her.

She closed her eyes and tried stifling her tears. It was hard to see the sun through the rain, but Leonard had a way about him that she trusted. He could tell her the stars were purple and she would be convinced that they were. This man was too good for her, and the frightening part was that suddenly she had the clarity to realize it. While Nadine recognized the attributes of a good man, she wasn't accustomed to the special treatment of being with one, which made her feel even more that she didn't deserve Leonard. Not with her track record. Not with her baggage.

"I'm not taking no for an answer. Allow me to help you. Please," he begged.

Uncontrollable tears raced down her cheeks. "Okay," she finally agreed, sniffling. "We'll follow you back to your place."

8

S abrina double-checked the doorknob to ensure she had locked it. She had. She quickly and quietly retrieved the turkey baster from her purse. She removed the Saran Wrap and stuck the instrument into her mouth. She squeezed the handle and vacuumed Jeff's semen into the tube, only filling it a third of the way. When it was all in there, she positioned herself on the edge of the commode, hiked her legs in the air, and inserted the tube as deeply inside her vagina as it would go. She squeezed the contents inside of her and remained in that uncomfortable position for at least five minutes. She pretended the knots in her stomach were his semen swimming through her maternal wards.

She rinsed the remnants of his cum from her tongue, teeth, and jaws. It was the first time she had ever allowed a man to ejaculate into her mouth. The first time! She hated herself for doing this, but she remembered her husband's words, *"We're doing this for our family."*

After freshening up, she walked back into the room. She located her clothes which were scattered all over the floor. Jeff was knocked out cold. As loud as he was snoring, he wouldn't have heard an atomic bomb detonate.

She quietly eased into her clothes. There was no need to stay the night. Her job here was more than done. After all, she was in Jeff's life for one reason and one reason only—a baby!

9

"I'm telling y'all, man, that chick was fine than a motherfucker! I started to put my girl and her shit outta my ride and make her ass walk the rest of the way home, just so I could turn around and holler at shorty!"

The entire barbershop erupted into hearty laughter as one of the barbers, J-Biz, shared his Friday's night account.

"You's a damn fool!" Canvas laughed along with everyone else, encouraging J-Biz.

J-Biz placed his right hand over his chest while holding the clippers in the left. "I ain't lying, y'all. I swear 'fo God, in all my twenty-seven years on this earth, I ain't never seen an ass that fat."

Jeff had only been in Canvas's chair for fifteen minutes and was already experiencing the camaraderie amongst the barbers at Precisionz Cuts. These fellas had no filters, but it felt damn good listening to someone else vent about their woman problems. He needed a laugh at someone's expense, if only to keep his mind off what was going on in his crazy world.

Kree, the barber at the end, slapped hands with J-Biz. "Nigga, you better than me. I would have actually done that shit. I would'a said, 'Sorry, shawty, but that's an ass I just can't pass.'" He laughed until he started choking. Jeff thought someone was going to have to perform the Heimlich maneuver on him until he finally recovered and yelled, "Ain't no pussy like some what...?"

"New pussy!" all the guys hollered in unison. At least everyone accept Jeff. He was totally occupied by trying to make sure Canvas didn't karate chop his hairline or peel his cap back. Stiff neck and all, his eyes were on the long mirror positioned directly across from them. It was the only mirror that had Canvas's name positioned vertically on the left side in black bold letters. When Jeff had seen that Canvas was the only barber with a mirror proclaiming who he was, paranoia settled in. Everybody knew that meant he was the new cat on the chopping block, aka fresh meat, aka the door greeter. Even had the first barber's chair next to the broken vending machine. That damn machine had stolen Jeff's money, and like a dummy, he had put in another dollar bill, thinking the wheel would turn properly the next try and release both bags of chips. When it didn't happen, everyone laughed at him and proceeded to introduce him to the barber shop's Piggy Bank. He'd learned rather quickly that it was a joke they played on all the new customers.

Innocently enough, the owner had grabbed him a bag of Doritos from the back room and returned one of his dollars. He had been officially initiated into the gang.

With all the excitement surrounding him, nerves still had his heart racing like an Amtrak and his armpits tingling. He didn't even blink out of trepidation that any sudden movement would somehow disturb Canvas's right-hand stroke, or better yet, block his good eye.

Heads turned toward the front door when it swung open. A brother no more than four feet tall, in suspenders, black slacks, and a black dress shirt with a yellow tie, walked in like he owned the spot, briefcase in hand.

"What's up, everybody?" he announced energetically.

"Just the man I've been waiting to see," one of the barbers in the back hollered out.

"All done with you, bro. Check me out," Canvas said to Jeff after spraying the oil sheen all over his fresh cut.

Jeff leaned slowly toward the mirror, his eyes in clear focus. He exhaled when he saw how precise his edge-up was. He carefully ran his palm over the top of his head. No plugs, no scalp maps. Canvas passed him a hand-held mirror and Jeff spun himself around to check out the back. He cracked a smile.

"All right, all right. I see ya," he said. "I ain't gon' lie though. You had a brother nervous as hell." He laughed heartily and so did Canvas.

"I told you I got you. Have more trust in a brother next time."

Jeff nodded his head. He went into his pocket and pulled out a twenty-dollar bill.

"Nah, man. I told you the first cut on me."

"You sure?" Jeff questioned.

Canvas nodded. "Positive."

"All right, Chief. That's what's up. Well, I'm gon' head on out of here and make some moves." He gave Canvas a fist pound. "If you don't have any plans tomorrow, you and your baby sister should come by the house. I'll teach you how to que."

"Barbeque!"

Jeff nodded.

Canvas beamed with excitement. "Yeaahhh…I might need to tighten my skills up a tad."

They shared a laugh.

"Bring your hooping shorts. I have a court in the backyard."

"Pssst. Man, you tryna get embarrassed on your own turf, huh?"

"Just for that ridiculous remark, I'm gon' have to wear that ass out. No mercy." He chuckled. He pulled a business card out of his wallet and jotted down his home address on the back.

Loaded with confidence, "We'll be there," Canvas said. "But don't say shit when I roast you on that court and make you eat your own words. I'm warning you right now, I'm cold with it." Canvas proceeded to sweep the hair up from around the chair.

"Yeah, we'll see about that." Jeff brushed off Canvas's arrogance and tittered as he removed the smock, laying it over the chair back.

Their attention turned in the other direction when suddenly everyone started hovering over the midget in the yellow tie. His briefcase was situated on his lap and the laptop on top of it. He had conveniently made himself an office right on the spot.

"What the hell y'all over here doing?" Canvas questioned as he joined the pack.

Jeff's curiosity was piqued as well but he had to go. This was his free Saturday. Deandra was with her grandmother, Grace, and his son was with Nadine. He was going to turn up tonight and he knew exactly who to send an invitation to.

"Drummer, you came through for your boy," J-Biz hollered excitedly. That smile was stretched so far across his wide face, Jeff had to walk over to see what all the hype was about.

Someone hollered, "Turn the volume up!"

Drummer raised the volume on his speaker, causing the loud moans to pour out for all in the barbershop to hear.

"You wanna fuck this tight, wet pussy?" a female voice asked. She flipped her hair to the side and that's when Jeff stuck his neck out to get a closer look. "I can do tricks unheard of." She moaned seductively.

"Go for it, baby!" one of the barbers clamored in Jeff's ear.

Jeff tensed up when the woman assumed the doggy-style position. He tilted his head to the side, his eyes not believing what was on that screen. He shook his head out of pure disgust and utter disbelief. He would recognize that pussy in a lineup.

She made her ass cheeks bounce. First the left cheek and then the right.

"Work it, baby!"

"Ooooh shit! Look at all that ass!" said another.

"Yo, I'm out," Jeff told Canvas whose eyes were fixated on the screen. Canvas bounced his head, never taking his eyes off the porn star.

Drummer paused the video and slapped his laptop closed. "End of preview, motherfuckers!" He laughed with his legs swinging in excitement.

"How much?" J-Biz's customer asked.

Drummer raised two DVDs in the air for all to lust over. "Fifteen will get you a date with China Doll, twenty will buy you Ménage. I also have the ones I showed y'all last week. I can let them go for twelve today. Cash only."

"Shit, let me grab that Ménage DVD. That tongue…wheewww… good Lawd o' mighty! Got a nigga seeing stars." The man cracked open his billfold, whipped out a fresh bill and passed it right to Drummer.

Jeff headed for the door, uninterested in supporting the panhandler or Ménage's thirsty ass.

"Say, my man," Drummer called after him. Jeff turned back in his direction. "You better grab you one of these hot joints while supplies last. They fresh off the press!"

Jeff shook his head. "Nah, bro. I'm good." He continued out the door as the other fellas churned out their money. He couldn't believe Ménage was making porn videos now. On second thought, he could believe it. She had always been a desperate type of chick willing to do anything for the green. Little did anyone know, seeing her on that video made him want to strangle her ass right through that screen.

He pulled his car keys out of his pocket and disarmed the alarm. He got in the car and attempted to start the engine. Before he could talk himself out of it, he hopped right back out and practically powerwalked the trail leading to the shop.

With a sense of urgency and waving a twenty-dollar-bill in Drummer's face, he said, "Let me go ahead and take that one off your hands, my man." His finger was pointed to the DVD case with Ménage's half naked ass on it.

"One Squirt Master coming right up." Drummer reached into his briefcase and swapped the money for the DVD. He held the bill up to the light, checking for its authenticity. Clearly satisfied with his findings, Drummer jammed the money in his pocket. "No refunds," he said quickly. "Here's my card. I can get you anything you need. Any time. Any day. Just holler at me. I'm your man." He tapped all ten fingers against his chest confidently.

Jeff gave him a head bounce. "Thanks. I'll bear that in mind."

Three-and-a-half hours later, Jeff was back at home. He fixed himself something to eat and retreated to his bedroom. With Ménage's sex tape in hand, he couldn't resist the temptation tugging at his dick. He hated that bitch with a passion, but it seemed his feelings were his and his only. His machinery felt a completely different way.

He turned off the lights, got comfortable, and popped in the flick. Had to see it with his own two eyes and on his own TV to believe it.

When Ménage's voluptuous round ass appeared on his seventy-inch flat screen, his rod instantly graduated several notches. Staying true to her stripper métier, she wore a sheer, peach-colored, strapless corset that exposed her pierced acorn-sized nipples. She had on a matching garter belt with no thong. Elongated pearls were double-roped and twisted around her neck, wrists, and ankles. The sight of it all conjured up old memories as Jeff assessed what used to be his weekend tradition. How could a woman he hated get his dick this excited?

He didn't waste any time calculating her every move. No matter what angle the director swung the camera in, Jeff knew every move and trick before it was even captured on film. It was simple after computing that he'd had sex with Ménage more times than what he had in his entire life. Even with his strong dislike for her, he smugly held on to that advantage.

The stripper-turned-porn star was in full swing. Her hairless pussy was spread eagle, torturing him with flashbacks. Now he wished they had made their own sex tape. Could have saved himself twenty dollars.

He continued to fight the urge wheedling him to pick up that phone and call her. He'd deal with the blame and shame later. *No, fuck that*, he thought. *I refuse to go back down that road.* Desperate to release the pressure rising in his tank, he quickly decided against the shorthand route. There was no way in hell he was beating his own stick when he had an assembly of pussies on speed dial. He placed his hand over his member in an attempt to calm it. When that didn't work, he turned off the television, snatched up his phone and dialed Sabrina's number. He hoped like hell her husband wasn't home.

"Hello," Sabrina answered on the third ring.

The minute she answered, Jeff asked her the question of the hour. "Is he there?"

She cleared her throat. Whispered, "Yes."

Jeff could hear the television in the background.

"Aghckkk! Aghckkk!"

Jeff almost aborted the call when her husband started coughing in the background, but once again, he thought about his sole purpose for the call.

"I'll grab you some water, honey."

"Thanks, baby."

Jeff could hear Sabrina making her exit, broadening that distance between her and her husband. Immediately he recognized his ranking. That acknowledgment only made him want her even more this instant, regardless of their circumstances and regardless of their unorthodox situation.

Sabrina's heels clattered across the floor in a series of swift steps. The rhythmic melody alluded to a feeling that surprisingly settled his temperamental dick, but he couldn't be sure how long that would last.

"I need to see you. Now," Jeff said, cutting straight to the chase.

"Now?" she questioned, apparently caught off guard by his frankness. It had taken Jeff by surprise as well, especially after avowing that he would not involve himself with her sexually again. He had pledged that if it didn't concern Deandra or dance, he wasn't going to entertain it. It was foolish, dangerous, and unfair to Sabrina. She deserved more than what he was willing to offer her. They all did.

Jeff looked back at the clock. It was only five o'clock. Still early. Enough time for her to rush over, serve him, then run back home to her husband before the football game went off. He didn't care how she arranged her time afterward, but it was his needs that needed seeing to right this moment.

"Yes. Now." He walked around the room and closed the curtains, instantly darkening the room.

As if reconsidering, Sabrina grew quiet. Too quiet for his comfort. He immediately began reprogramming his mind. Christie wouldn't be this difficult. He wouldn't have to persuade her to come over and jump on his train. Sensing Sabrina's hesitation, he chided himself for not phoning his main booty call first.

"What am I going to tell Luke?" Sabrina asked finally.

"I don't know. Get creative like you always do."

"Tsk. That helps a lot."

Answering to her husband was *her* problem, not his. Jeff wasn't the one with a ring on his finger. No obligations. No commitments. No dick-on-lockdown. Again, not his headache.

"I'll try to figure something out," she said quietly.

Jeff shook his head, already initiating his backup plan. Christie responded immediately to his coded text message. He almost ditched Sabrina so that he could hop in the shower and ride out. Just as he was about to cancel his proposition, she started up again.

"I'll be there shortly. I'll tell him I need to take some dance music to a student. He'll buy that." She sounded confident and convincing enough that Jeff's next text to Christie was asking her to be on standby.

"Do whatever you gotta do. Don't keep me waiting."

"So we're making demands now, Mr. Jackson?"

"You already know what time it is. I shouldn't have to beg for it...but I will."

"Ummm...I must admit, I'm intrigued. Should I wear something spontaneous?" Seduction laced her voice and Jeff played right along.

"No. I don't want to see you wearing anything. Nothing at all."

10

Sabrina lowered the phone from her ear. When she turned her heels, Luke was standing directly in front of her. She jumped.

"Gosh. You startled me."

"You're such a good little liar."

"It was Jeff," she admitted.

"Of course it was. Who else would be calling my wife for a *booty call*," he tittered wryly. "That is what they still call it nowadays, isn't it?"

He took the bottle of water from her hand, twisted the cap off, and gulped it all down. Snatching his eyes off of her, he tossed the bottle in the trash. He casually strolled back down the long hallway which led to a spacious study, leaving Sabrina utterly dumbfounded and confused. Why was he suddenly referring to their arrangement as booty calls? How dare he disrespect her! How dare he mock her like some slut! She took right after him, occasionally sweeping her voluptuous bouncing curls out of her face.

Luke was right where she suspected he would be. He had abandoned the football game altogether and was plopped down directly in front of the computer. As of late, it was what seemed to hold his interest the most. She was starting to question what was so important but quickly chided herself for it. She was certain he was spending all this excessive time online looking for employment. It was where he had discovered opportunities in the past.

She stood right at the doorway boring holes through his body with her gleaming eyes. Seemingly unfazed by her sudden intrusion and silence, Luke proceeded to retrieve a notepad and calculator from the desk.

So he's just going to sit there and ignore me? "Booty call, Luke?" Sabrina spat defiantly. If he didn't know, he was aware now that he had struck a major nerve.

"Ha, ha, ha. For God's sake, I was only kidding." He met her unforgiving glare.

"Does it look like I'm laughing?" she retorted.

Luke shrugged his shoulders as if there wasn't necessarily anything to apologize for. He dismissively cut his eyes, planting his skinny, languid fingers back onto the keyboard.

She took a deep breath, trying her best to speak civilly with him to avoid an argument.

"I didn't realize from six years ago up until now that my wife had lost her sense of humor in between."

Her face scrunched with pure disdain. "I haven't. But sometimes you can be so fucking insensitive. Here I am sniffing behind another man's penis just to please you," she spat icily, "and you're the one treating me as though I'm the neighborhood whore!"

Luke did a full swing in the chair, facing her. "Well, quite frankly, I thought you were starting to revel in all the time you've been spending with him," he retorted.

Luke's aloofness alluded to the asshole of a husband Sabrina felt he had become. It was why some days she wanted out of the marriage and out of his life. He changed drastically after the motorcycle accident and she was the first to notice. The therapist had warned her that it would take time for him to accept the damage that had been done in order for him to heal himself mentally, but Sabrina didn't realize she would be a significant key to the process.

And while Sabrina saw how difficult it was at times for her husband, she felt she had the greater challenge of catering to his insecurities and sexual dysfunctions.

"You thought I was starting to revel in the time I've been spending with him…what the hell is that supposed to mean?" Sabrina charged.

Luke relaxed his shoulders, took a deep breath, and in a single motion roughly combed his fingers in frustration through his neatly styled hair. "It means nothing," he said after a long pause.

"No, say what's on your mind! Go ahead and admit what we both already know."

She walked closer to him so that she could look deeply into his eyes. She already knew the answer but she wanted to hear it from Luke. He had been acting real funny lately and this explained why. He was jealous. Jealous and scared that she would leave him for Jeff. Right when she thought he was about to admit that he wanted her to stop seeing Jeff, his eyes tore away from her, robbing her of that moment of truth.

"I'll be glad when this is over, that's all. I don't like this any more than you do. And just so we're clear, I would not have allowed this if I didn't envision the bigger picture," he said, staring at the computer screen the entire time.

She tenderly reached for his chin and turned his face in her direction, hoping to reestablish their connection. Her eyes pleaded with him. "Say the word, Luke, and I will put an end to it. There has to be another way to do this. We can both figure it out."

Luke shook his head. "No," he said calmly. Sabrina's hand brushed the collar of his shirt as she pulled back. "We started it; we're going to finish it. It's only a matter of time before you're pregnant with our baby, again."

She averted her eyes, a sense of regret strangling her silent. She walked off with nothing more to say, surprised that he didn't call after her as he usually did after an unsettling disagreement. Her feet moved quickly but quietly across the Victorian ingrain carpeting that sectioned off all the main rooms in the house, including the study and the great room. It was that dreadful ornamental trail that reminded her daily of the little old woman whose house they had squattered. With that hanging over her head, Sabrina shamefully acknowledged that their time was running out.

She retreated to her own private sanctuary. Once in the bathroom, she ditched her oatmeal-colored leggings, her cream blouse, bra and panties. She suddenly felt like her husband's dirty little whore. How in the world did they go from living without a care in the world to lying and scheming innocent people? As much as she wanted to put an end to it, her love for Luke always managed to combat her resistance. He desperately wanted another baby and had found the perfect candidate to make that happen. She constantly told herself that Jeff was nothing more than a benefactor. Once he knocked her up, she would never have to see or hear from him again.

Sabrina's mind took her elsewhere as she quickly showered and prepped for a session with Jeff. Her moment of solitude sparked an idea that nearly scared her half to death. It was risky, but if she played her cards right, she and Luke could have the baby, the money, and the perfect start to a normal life once again.

Sabrina sent Jeff a text message informing him that she was pulling out of her driveway. Minutes later, she rounded the block in the cherry-red Volkswagen Beetle her baby sister, Ashley, had loaned her. It was supposed to have been temporary, but she'd had the car almost a year now because she and Luke were still financially strapped. Ashley had been the only one Sabrina had confided in after her and Luke's matching Range Rovers were repossessed. She hadn't even told her parents that they had lost everything: they were homeless, broke, and covered in debt up to their hairlines. It was too embarrassing to admit so she never uttered a word about it. Sabrina had even asked Ashley not to open her mouth either. Surprisingly so, the spoiled college brat could keep a secret. Though every now and then Ashley would remind Sabrina of how she was several states away, at college, with no transportation. It had only made Sabrina feel worse.

If their parents ever found out, Sabrina would never hear the end of it. They would see her as the failure they proclaimed she was since the day she dropped out of high school. She had gotten knocked up by her on-again-off-again boyfriend, and when she told him she was three months' pregnant with twins, he dropped her like a bad habit. Her bourgeois, judgmental parents had been right about him all along, and while they had taken her to the abortion clinic to get rid of *her* problem, consequently their parent-child relationship was never the same after that. She had only gone through the abortion to satisfy them and had to live with that regret every single day.

Sabrina whipped around the corner and pulled onto Jeff's street. She brought the car to a stop directly in front of his house. She wasn't surprised to find the porch light off and his car conveniently parked in the middle of the driveway, taking up both sides and leaving her no choice but to park at the curb. It wasn't unusual. She had driven by the house many of nights and observed the same thing. Perhaps it was his way of letting her know not to get too comfortable, which she hadn't planned to anyhow. Men were so fucking predictable. Thought they controlled everything, when in actuality, they were only as smart as women allowed them to be.

She rounded her car and walked the dim trail of lights neatly positioned along the pathway leading to his porch. When she arrived at his door, she slowly turned the knob to see if he had left it unlocked. He had. She walked right into the darkness, locking the door behind her.

Sabrina pulled her long, tailored, black pea coat snugly across her chest as she headed for his bedroom. The spikey heels of her black suede thigh-high boots announced her presence, but he couldn't have heard the introduction over Tank's song "Close" playing in the background. She eased the bedroom door open. The red and black curtains were pulled to, the matching satin bed sheets on his king-sized bed were peeled midway, and a strawberry fragrance burned from across the room. The mood was purposefully set. She was surprised he had put any thought at all into creating such romantic illusion. She looked to her right and witnessed the steam escaping the bathroom. It was her cue to get right to business.

She quickly undressed, ready to get this over with so that she could get back to her husband. She laid her things over the chair and when she turned back around, she spotted the two gold packs on the nightstand. Her eyes combed the room desperately until finally landing on an empty plate. The plate was useless, but the fork would get the job done.

In full motion, she took the utensil and punctured several discreet holes into both condom packs. When she was satisfied, she replaced the fork back onto the plate and walked calmly into the bathroom. All she and Luke wanted from this man was a baby. The second the test confirmed that she was pregnant, her mission would be complete, and she and Luke could move forward with their lives.

She joined Jeff in the vastly large marble stand-up shower, which was adjacent to the walk-in closet. It was a sandy brown and cream marble and large enough to fit a twin-sized bed inside of it. It made her miss the smallest luxuries of her and Luke's mini mansion. Made her want her old life back even more.

Clad in his birthday suit, her eyes locked on his lathered body as the water made a river trail down his chocolate chiseled torso. Her knees nearly buckled in anticipation.

"Bring your sexy ass over here," Jeff beckoned. His anaconda, which seemingly hung longer than an elephant's trunk between his legs, whispered her name right behind that. She didn't know who to answer to first.

Biting down on her bottom lip, she walked over to him. Their bodies intertwined and the masculine scent of his body wash entranced her, interrupting her previous train of thought. He didn't need to know that her heart was racing like a turbo engine. Didn't need to know that her sweet wet pussy had memorized every digit of his love offering and had already lubed itself accordingly.

His kisses fell hungrily across her lips as the water rushed down like raining pellets, slapping against their bare skin. The attraction and desire to be fucked senseless was inexorable. He was a handsome, well-endowed man who knew every curve and crevice of a woman's anatomy; gifted and fully equipped in areas her husband was not, or had ever been. She couldn't hide from that fact if she tried. But it almost made her hate him. Hate him for not being Luke.

Jeff's manly hands cupped her neck before falling evenly over her shoulder blades in the most sensual caress. Every kiss he swept across her skin had intentionally set her pussy on fire. It became harder to breathe. Harder to think.

"I've been waiting on this all day," he told her.

"Oh, really. I'm surprised last night hadn't been enough." He landed another kiss on her chin. Her lips.

"I could never have too much of this."

"Careful now." She moaned. "They say too much of a good thing can be bad on the heart."

His lips fell short on a response, but his eyes said it all. They rechanneled that toxic energy consuming her and slowly converted her to his side. Suddenly, she craved more. Demanded more. She no longer wanted to just be fucked and sent home. No, she wanted *everything* this man had to offer.

Long, thick fingers steadily climbed her body, leaving a trail for warm passionate kisses to follow suit. Her hands set out on their own adventure, gliding sensually along his stiff chocolate opus. She moved to his sexual frequency, desiring him in unimaginable ways. Then slowly, she came to, remembering why she was here. Caught up in the rapture, she immediately reprimanded herself for even thinking past this minute, this hour...realizing that anything that felt this easy, this perfect, was intangible. It was all part of the façade she had helped to create. It was no secret that Jeff had his smokescreen up. With all that had happened to him in the past, she couldn't blame him. But sadly enough, his bouts with women weren't enough to earn her sympathy and cause her to abort her mission.

Playing her role, Sabrina began to stroke him. To embrace and encourage him to fuck her and make it worth her while. He responded instantaneously. Jeff slowly backed her against the wall. He clamped his large hand around both her wrists and pinned them above her head, against the sweaty marble. His long and dedicated tongue hungrily whipped across her engorged nipples before he could squeeze his lips around them. His free hand impatiently explored alternate avenues, easing two fingers inside of her, one at a time.

"Ummmmm!" Sabrina moaned as a tingling sensation shot through her vertebrae, each thrust of his fingers wheedling her to a premature climax. "Not yet," she begged. "I need you inside of me."

At her request, Jeff slowly withdrew. She opened her eyes just in time to see him licking his coated fingers as if that was the vitamin C he'd been waiting on all day. He hoisted her in the air, kissing her all the way to the sit-in bench. He sat her down on that wet, smooth surface, and claimed a front row seat between her thighs. Squatted before her, he parted her legs and tongue-kissed the skin between her legs. Her hair clung to her face, neck and back, but he only opted to clear the piece of hair blocking her sight. It was though he didn't want her to miss any part of the action. He pulled her to the edge of the bench and lowered his face into her beckoning pussy, kissing it, caressing it, and claiming it as his own.

Sabrina's head practically fell off her shoulders from the mere touch of his proficient tongue cuddling her folds. Her eyes drifted to the back of her head and Jeff must have taken notice to shift the way he did. She reopened them and watched as he buried his tongue deeper into her orifice, prompting a sound to escape her that her own ears couldn't identify with.

"Oh, Jeff!" Sabrina called out hoarsely in satisfaction. Jeff didn't relent, only quickened his pace. He flicked his tongue insanely against her clit, driving and provoking her to scream, "Fuck me!" To be sure he'd heard her clearly the first time, she shouted the words again.

Immersed in their own sexual synergy, Jeff rose from between her legs on her command. Her lips trembled in aftershock as her first true climax of tonight, reverberated the fireworks sounding off inside of her. He kissed her quivering lips, calming them. As though he didn't want to spare another minute, he pulled Sabrina to her feet. On one sexual accord, she propped one leg onto the bench. He slowly entered her, filling her up.

"Oh yes, fuck me!" she cried out.

"Fuck you like this?" Jeff asked, staring into her eyes. Her silence was brought on by every lethal stroke drilling a wider and deeper hole inside her pussy. Sabrina nearly lost it. Her breathing intensified and she quaked in response as he drove himself in and out of her in slow, deep strokes. He hugged her breasts, sucking them simultaneously in between thrusts. "Or fuck you like this?" He pivoted them in reverse and got a better grip on his balance while still nestled inside of her. She pushed her back more toward the shower wall for leverage. She wrapped her legs loosely around his tight ass as he held her up by the back of her thighs. Her breasts were smothered against his chest as he pushed himself to her maximum. She cried out in both pleasure and pain. Jeff bent back slightly to enhance his performance. The shift change had him perfectly angled. She clenched her muscles, heightening the tension. She was on the verge of cumming again. It was the first time a man had ever hit her G-spot.

Sabrina could feel her hair tangle somewhere along her spine, but she didn't care. This was well worth it. He gripped her waist even tighter and her breasts bounced freely as he slammed his pelvis into hers.

"I'm almost there!" she panted, skating her own fingers across her nipples while he plowed into her.

"Cum on my dick." He smacked her on the bottom, chanting those same words all over again.

"Agggghhh!" Sabrina cried in wicked pleasure, doing exactly as she was told.

Jeff quickly withdrew himself, turned off the shower and carried her into the bedroom. He laid her across the bed and hurriedly tore open one of the condoms situated on the nightstand. He blindly slipped it over his erection and once he was completely inside of her, she squeezed her walls around him, forcing him to cum deeply inside of her. He shook vigorously on top of her as he released his baby-making seeds right onto her golden pathway.

It was three o'clock in the morning when Sabrina turned back on her street. She had no intentions on staying at Jeff's place this late. No intentions at all. She calmly walked into the house, expecting Luke to be waiting up for her, but hoping he was not. Although they were in this together, she refused to disparage him by flaunting it in his face. It was why she always left the room whenever Jeff called. Why she didn't tell Luke any of the sordid details. It would only complicate things even further. He didn't need to know that she enjoyed Jeff's attention; that he was the greatest lover she ever had; that she wished she had met him before Luke. She had deemed those details worthless. All he needed to know was that soon enough, she would be having *their* baby.

She made a beeline for the bedroom and found him sleeping soundlessly in her spot. She was too tired to shower. Too tired to do anything but remove her coat and boots. She took the quickest shower she had ever taken, brushed her teeth, then climbed in the bed naked beside Luke. Out of habit, he wrapped his arms around her. She could feel his breath on the back of her neck.

"That was a pretty late party," Luke said.

Sabrina quickly turned to face him. "I thought you were asleep."

Luke's piercing eyes were glossed over. He shook his head. "It's impossible to sleep easy when my wife's not lying beside me."

She nestled more closely to him. "I'm here now, baby," she murmured, kissing him on the lips and brushing his hair with her fingers. "And I'm not going anywhere," she added convincingly before drifting off to sleep in his arms.

11

It was nights like this when Leonard would relax in his recliner and immerse himself in his own private world. He had been at the hospital for the majority of the day and hadn't really had the opportunity to lend his thoughts to anything else besides his best friend. Now, sitting here alone, reminded him that there was still some unfinished business. He had to figure out how he was going to tell Nadine his innermost secret. He worried that she would leave and never look back. They all did. That's why telling the woman he had fallen deeply in love with that he was HIV positive was one of the hardest things he ever had to do.

Leonard knew from the first day he laid eyes on Nadine that he was in love. He had never believed in love at first sight until he encountered his striking and amazing girlfriend. One might consider it pure happenstance how they met. Not him. Chance was finding a suitcase full of money or avoiding rush-hour traffic on the commute to work. Chance was the absence of obvious design. This here was much greater than that. It was God intervening and blessing him with what he had always prayed for—a wife. Never had he fallen this quickly for a woman, which is why he knew Nadine was nothing of the ordinary. She was a rare find. So many nights he cried alone, praying that God would send him a woman who would love him beyond his current situation. A woman who would look past his imperfections and love him for him. Unconditionally. That's the kind of woman he had reserved his heart for. And the more he got to know Nadine, the more he realized that she was his soulmate. She gave him a glimmer of hope that a sero-discordant relationship could very well be functional and realistic on the basis of consistent true love.

Leonard thought he would be all alone for the night until he heard the steps creak. He peered over his shoulder and smiled when he saw Nadine descending the stairs, wearing one of his blue button-down shirts. Her radiant butterscotch skin seemingly lit up his otherwise dark loft as she moved quietly in his direction, exhibiting acres of enchanting Nubian flesh. She was his queen and didn't even know it. To breathe the same air as her reaffirmed his purpose with renewed conviction that he too could experience true happiness. Love would prevail and allow her to see past his ailment. It had to.

"Can't sleep," she confessed, getting comfortable on the couch. "Is the mattress okay?"

She nodded. "It's perfect." She inhaled deeply before releasing a long sigh. "I…have a lot on my mind."

Leonard had been watching an episode of *The Jeffersons* before she came down. It was one of his favorite television classics of all time. But her being in his presence warranted his undivided attention. He lowered the volume, placed the remote on the table, and claimed a spot right beside her.

"Is there anything I can do to ease your mind?" Her eyes traveled to his groin. "Besides *that*." He chuckled, dismissing her innuendo.

She smiled innocuously and placed a hand inside of his.

"You're already doing more than enough." Her smile boosted his spirits. It always did. She snuggled next to him and turned her attention toward the TV. He could get used to having a woman around the house. He was always up for good company; besides, it would be the perfect opportunity to get to know her better, of course that was if she would give him the chance to. But since Leonard was also a realist, he suspected that after tonight, things were bound to take a sharp turn.

They shared a laugh as they watched George and Louise debate over whether or not to hire a replacement for their maid, Florence. Her laughter humbled him. Made him grateful for the simplest things like moments like this where he could cuddle with his woman and be entertained by reruns all night. Moments where merely existing and breathing in each other's space was enough to send his rocket to the moon. Moments where nothing outside of that door mattered. Nothing.

Damn, why me? he thought gravely, his mind racing from one thing to the next. Suddenly, the television was a distraction. It was time he cleared the air while he had the perfect opportunity to do so. He needed to tell her exactly how he felt about her and why he would understand if she couldn't handle his situation. It wouldn't be fair to force this on her. It was his battle and his alone. As depressing as it was, that much he had come to grips with.

When Leonard first learned he had contracted the virus three years ago, he was angry. He was in denial and in shock after receiving the diagnosis, so much so that he'd requested to have the test readministered, only to reach the same findings. His entire life had virtually been altered in the blink of an eye. He had obsessed over how his family and friends would react. How it might affect his business dealings and potential relationships if anyone ever found out. Most of all, he became angry at the idea that he would never have children of his own. He hadn't done anything to deserve a death sentence, he recalled thinking. He had been the faithful and devoted man his parents raised him to be. He had never in his life cheated on a woman, or anything for that matter, not even his taxes. Not once. But he knew no one would ever believe that he had indeed contracted the virus from the very woman whom he had been engaged to marry. The biggest misconception associated with HIV was that a woman likely contracted it from some cheating man. He was living proof that that wasn't always the case.

Coming from a rather large family, getting married and starting a family of his own were goals for him. His mother loved children and Leonard had promised to give her at least ten grandbabies. Give or take six. Real big dreams. His future had been all mapped out, right down to the family road trips they would take. Seemingly overnight, all those big dreams had been shattered before he ever had the chance to say "I do." Chasity Givens, the woman whom he had loved and cherished, had robbed him of his future to a great degree. He would never know or understand why his love hadn't been enough for her; she had died unexpectedly due to heart complications. It was only then when he discovered that she was knowingly infected. Hours after her passing, he had learned that she had passed the virus to him.

Being fully committed to the woman he chose to share his life with, he never expected HIV to lay claim on his life, and when it did, he had no choice but to deal with it the best way he knew how. There were only two options—live or die. He chose to live. But the staunch stigma and discrimination that people with HIV experienced was real, which was more the reason why he feared rejection from any woman he tried dating seriously. He had only known Nadine for six weeks, but in that short amount of time, he knew deep down that she was the one. He could feel it. He only prayed that she didn't look at him any differently after he disclosed his status, but he knew the odds were stacked against him.

As she nestled her head against him, something within encouraged him to act. Had his worry not been triggered from past repudiation, he would have followed his true intentions and told her on day one. But those relationships had taught him not to be so forthcoming. So in order to protect his own heart, he decided he would wait until *he* was ready to reveal his truth, and that time was now. She deserved to know before they went any further. Before he admitted how deeply in love he was with her.

The Jeffersons went off and it went straight to a commercial. Leonard muted the volume before paranoia could cloud his mind space.

"Baby, I need to talk to you about something."

Nadine raised her head, worry in her beautiful brown eyes. There was no easy way to say this, but he had to purge this secret he'd been safeguarding. He couldn't allow her to continue a relationship with him to only be blindsided by the truth. He would never want to deceive her so he had to fix this now or deal with the consequences later.

"What I'm about to say isn't easy for me," he confessed, his tone low.

She touched the side of his face tenderly. "Me first."

12

It was now or never. This was the only reason Nadine had worked up the nerve to come downstairs and finally get this plaguing ghost of guilt off her chest. She paced herself, although she had already practiced exactly what she would say the second he walked through that door. There was no way she could live under his roof without being completely honest with him about her past, especially not after learning that Greg Adams was his best friend. The truth would surely come out someday, and she preferred him to get it directly from her.

Her stomach knotted as she sat there contemplating how to begin. There was no easy way to say it, but she had to manage her choice of words and pray a careful delivery would soften the blow.

"I want you to know that I care about you so much," she started out. "I never thought that I would fall for a man so quickly." Tears misted her bright brown eyes. "But I…haven't been completely truthful with you."

Leonard's stoic expression coaxed her into continuing.

"Your friend, Greg…was a former client of mine." She paced herself, easing into this without deliberately sabotaging their budding relationship. "My best friend, Denise, the one I told you all about…" Leonard nodded, pulling her closer into his embrace. He must have known this was difficult for her. She wondered how long his compassion would stick around after what she was about to reveal. Nadine finally let those tears go. "She had introduced me to Greg, and at that time, I wasn't aware of their relationship." She took a deep breath. "Denise was Jeff's wife."

"Jeff? Canvas's father, Jeff?" he clarified.

"Yes." She had his full attention. This was difficult, but she had come too far to stop.

Leonard shifted in his seat, wiping indiscernible beads of sweat from his chocolate bald head.

"I had an affair with my best friend's husband during the time she was cheating on him with Greg."

"Greg was...*is*...married," Leonard added.

She nodded her affirmation. Filled with angst, her eyes never wavered.

"I am not proud of what I did. I have lived with this every day, and I grow disgusted whenever I think about the role I played in that relationship." He wiped away the tears plummeting her cheeks. "I'm not perfect," she admitted. "I have prayed for forgiveness... and I have vowed to never make those mistakes again." She dropped her head and allowed the tears to fall on the tail of his shirt.

He gently rubbed her back. "It's okay. Let it all out."

She slowly raised her head again. Stared at him. She wished she knew what was going through his mind. "I hope this doesn't change how you feel about me," she said dimly.

"Not at all." He lifted her chin slightly and rested his eyes on hers. "Listen to me. I realize we haven't known each other that long, but I'm already in love with you, Nadine. Your past is your past, and that's where it's going to stay. It doesn't ever have to come up again."

Her throat became clogged from the tears spilling from her heart. What had she done to deserve this man in her life?

"I will always be here for you," he continued. "I love you."

"I love you, too." They kissed softly and he wrapped his arms around her. In that moment her mind felt more at ease. She nestled her head underneath his chin until she was able to hear his heart thumping through his chest. Her eyes soon landed on a picture of him cutting the red ribbon at the grand opening of his restaurant, Chasity's. She loved a hardworking man that held things down on his own. "Now what was it that you wanted to talk to me about?"

Leonard cleared his throat and raised up from his position. "Ummm…Greg's vitals have improved."

"That's great news!"

"Yeah." He paused. "The road to recovery won't be easy though."

Nadine listened intently.

"Doctors are saying it's a strong possibility he's going to have to learn to walk, talk, read, write…everything, all over again."

Her mouth dropped in surprise. "Oh, I am so sorry to hear that." She could tell this was difficult for him. He looked straight ahead, rejecting that tear that she saw hanging in the corner of his left eye. This time she rubbed his back and looped her arm around his. They were each other's comforter. He was there for her during this stressful time and she was happy that she could be there for him during his time of need.

"Yeah, it'll get better. God is in full control."

"Amen to that."

Nadine and Leonard talked for what felt like hours. He shared childhood stories of how he and Greg grew up and how he had been the best man in Greg's wedding. He shared how they had tried just about every business venture under the sun. She also learned that it was Greg who had invested in Leonard's restaurant. The more Leonard talked about his friend, the more he seemed to light up from reminiscing on all the good times they shared. It made her think more and more about Denise. She missed her so much. If she could turn back the hands of time, she would tell her how much their friendship meant to her; how sorry she was for betraying her; how much she loved her. But it was too late. She would never get to say those words.

When it was time to call it a night, Leonard walked her back upstairs. Before she could climb into bed, he grabbed her by the hand and did something no man she had ever dated did in her presence. He knelt beside the bed and gestured for her to join him. As he bowed his head and placed his hands in a prayer fold, she practically venerated him as a saint from that moment on. She closed her eyes and he began to pray.

In the midst of her storm, Leonard Dupree was her ray of sunlight. He was the most humble, modest, and loving black man she knew. He was perfect. Perfect for her. Perfect for her son. She smiled peacefully as she dozed off to sleep. Jeff Jackson was slowly becoming history.

13

Wednesday, September 24th

After her consultation with the attorney two days ago, Naomi was even more thrilled about starting her new life as Denise Adams. She never imagined the process would be so tedious, which is why she decided to let her new attorney handle all the filings with the court on her behalf. She had supplied her with everything she needed right along with a hefty bonus to expedite things. She had learned from both Greg and Maribel that money could procure anything, including a brand-new life. She could hardly believe that only a few years ago she was homeless, begging and prostituting for money. Well, not anymore. She now had a beautiful brick mansion in an affluent Los Angeles neighborhood, millions of dollars, stocks, bonds, a new image, and a clean slate. All she needed to complete her happily-ever-after was her husband, Greg.

Naomi never stopped loving Greg, despite Maribel's admission that she and Greg had chosen to reconcile. It pained Naomi to know that Greg didn't have the balls to tell her himself, but after all, Maribel was his wife. Vivian, Maribel…Naomi couldn't help but wonder what other moniker his wife had used to manipulate and deceive in order to get her way. And while Naomi's hands were just as dirty, Greg had every right to know the truth. She couldn't imagine that he would still want to be married to that crazed wench after learning that she had hired Naomi during her quest to destroy him.

Naomi painfully realized that a future with Greg was slim to nothing, but she had to hold on to the little bit of hope she managed to preserve. Ultimately, it was the major role in that deceptive guise Maribel had concocted that lured Greg to Naomi. If it weren't for her strong resemblance to Denise Jackson, his deceased mistress, Greg likely would not have taken immediate interest. He was a distinguished man with exceptional taste, high standards, class, power, and money. He could have had any woman he wanted. Yet behind the mask Naomi wore, he had unknowingly fallen for a recovering alcoholic who had been battling that same fight his own wife had. Naomi was foolish for even thinking he would recover from that grim revelation, but she held on to that last ounce of hope. Every passionate moment they shared together, had to have meant more than *sex*. At least, that's what her heart coaxed her to believe.

Roaming the second floor of her beautiful abode in a silk, champagne-gold-and-black Kimono bathrobe, Naomi looked, smelled, and felt like royalty. Her freshly pedicured feet graced the luxurious thirty-thousand-dollar rug along the corridor. Feeling larger than life, she paused periodically to envision how it would look once her interior decorator added the finishing touches. She could not wait for the rest of the furniture she'd ordered to arrive. It was going to make the home even more impeccable than it already was.

She leisurely descended the spiral staircase, coasting her hand along the custom-made railing and enjoying the breathtaking view. From the glints of gold in the crown molding, the fancy ceiling medallion and crystal chandeliers to the ivory-coffee marble floors, this was simply heaven on earth, and it was all hers. She moseyed through the foyer, her stomach growling along the journey. The kitchen screamed her name, but when she opened the refrigerator, her options were limited to three slices of leftover pepperoni pizza and an enchilada TV dinner. She frowned at the reminder that she needed to make a trip to the grocery store. She poured a glass of milk to settle her until she could make the time to go. She would kill for her mother's meatloaf right now. The very thought brought her to pause. She hadn't spoken to her family in two whole years, and every time she attempted to reach out, she could not bring herself to make the call. They had been so judgmental toward her, condemning her for her alcohol addiction. They had abandoned her during her time of need, and Naomi had yet to forgive them for that. Little did they know, she was a changed woman now with brand-new shoes and a new attitude.

A smile crossed her lips as she thought about how they would react if they saw her now, living like this. With her past behind her and a new lease on life, Naomi was ready to face her family again. She missed her children dearly, and it broke her heart to think about letting another day go by without hearing their voices or seeing their faces. She would have to make amends with Charles sooner or later, for the sake of their children.

An unexpected thought struck her and she rushed over to the island and rummaged through her purse. She whipped out her new cell phone, climbed on one of the bar stools and dialed the number from memory. She prayed that it hadn't changed. Tears welled up in her eyes as she mentally struggled, unsure of what to say.

"Hello," a woman's weak and raspy voice answered on the fourth ring.

"Mama? This is Naomi!" She pulled the phone tighter to her ear, smiling at the sound of the comforting voice on the other end of the line.

"Naomi…?"

"Yes, it's me, Mama. Your daughter."

The voice on the other end grew quiet.

"I…I thought you were dead."

Tears poured down Naomi's face. If her mother thought she was dead, surely her children had thought the same thing.

"I hadn't heard from you, Charles hadn't heard from you." She paused. "We all…thought you were dead."

Naomi could barely breathe as that heavy burden of guilt plopped on her chest.

"Where are you? Are you still sick?" her mother drilled.

"No, I'm fine, Ma," Naomi said, quickly putting her mother's mind at ease. "I'm in full recovery," she volunteered.

She could hear her mother's heavy breathing. "Good…good. Well, at least one of us is in full recovery."

"What do you mean, Mama?" Naomi's brows furrowed.

"Baby, they've diagnosed your mama with breast cancer."

Naomi's hand flew to her chest. She was confounded. "Breast cancer?" She could barely utter the words.

"Doctors say it's progressed and that there's nothing more they can do."

"No…no…there has to be something they can do." Her heart quickened as she headed back upstairs. Her feet plodded along the long trail to her bedroom. She headed straight for the closet, pulling out one of several Louis Vuitton suitcases.

"The chemotherapy ain't done shit but take out all my hair and zap what little bit of life I had left out of me. And the pain…it's become so unbearable that the nurse keeps me doped up on all this morphine."

Naomi only stopped to allow herself time to regain her strength. The mere thought of losing her mother brought her to her knees.

She sat in the middle of the floor, doubled over with tears racing down her face.

"But don't you worry about me. I'm just glad to know you're alive and well. God must have heard my final request." She moaned weakly.

"I'm coming to get you, Mama. You can come live with me," Naomi interjected, her voice cracking along the way. "You'll have your own room and your own private doctor to look after—"

"Whoa, whoa, whoa…slow down with all that nonsense. Chile, you'se talking like you done struck it rich or something," her mother tittered despicably. "And even if you have, I'm not leaving my home. Your father died in my arms, right in this very bed I'm lying in. I can still feel his spirit here next to me." A quietness filled the phone line. "I'm never leaving Billy," she professed. "So when God feels He's ready for me, He'll know exactly where to find me. And only until then will I leave this room."

14

As soon as the plane touched down, Naomi lifted her head and stared out the window. She was back in Dallas, Texas. Back where it all started. She pulled the black and gold-trimmed Vera Wang Eudora shades from her face and tucked them inside her purse. The young Asian woman seated next to her smiled when their elbows collided.

"Excuse me, I'm so sorry," Naomi apologized, realizing that she hadn't been paying attention to what she was doing.

The woman pulled the earphones from her ears. "It's okay," she politely replied. Her thin lips curved into a warm genuine smile.

The flight attendant came over the intercom and Naomi took out the time to fold the midsize blanket they had given her and to get her head together. Her sole purpose for returning to Texas was to see after her terminally ill mother, and hopefully, reestablish a relationship with her children in the process of family bonding. She had not reached out or spoken to anyone in years, but it was time that she came out of hiding. They all had thought she was dead, but what pained her the most was knowing that no one bothered to look for her. The rift between her and her family had kept her out of sight and out of mind, and sadly enough, it might have been for the best.

After deboarding the airplane, Naomi followed the signs and walked straight ahead and in the direction to retrieve her luggage from baggage claim. She had only brought along two suitcases, figuring she could always by more clothes during her stay if it were necessary. But her agenda was laid out before she stepped foot on that plane. She had every intention on convincing her mother to move to Los Angeles with her so that she could look after her more closely and get her the help she needed, no matter the cost. She refused to believe there was no hope. Refused to believe that her mother was dying from stage IV breast cancer.

As she hauled her luggage through the airport searching for a car rental dealer, the smell of freshly brewed coffee seduced her senses. She had not had one bite to eat and her stomach was turning flips and doing the most as a result. She followed the trail which led her right to a small cafe. Instead of her usual she opted for a chai tea latte. Big mistake. She rushed back to exchange the drink for something more appeasing to her taste buds. After receiving her new beverage, she resumed her pursuit for a rental car.

"Welcome to Enterprise!" someone behind the counter greeted enthusiastically when Naomi entered the store. "What kind of vehicle can I get for you today?"

Naomi returned the attendant's smile as she walked up to the counter. Upon closer inspection, she realized the voice of the stockily built greeter with the bald fade, actually belonged to a woman. Besides her low-cut and boyish persona, she represented a rainbow bracelet on her left wrist, but it was her name that gave her away. She didn't know too many men whose parents had named them Felecia.

"What do you have available?" Naomi asked, trying not to make it obvious that she was staring.

"We have a pretty good selection to choose from. Are you looking for a compact, mid-size, or luxury vehicle? Let me add that we have the best rate in this airport so you can't go wrong." She leaned over the counter. "I'd take advantage of the swag car special," she whispered.

Swag car special? "All right, I'll take that one." Naomi met the woman's smile and curiosity immediately took hold of her. She had always wondered how lesbians "do it," but she sure as hell wasn't trying to find out. She diverted her attention and watched a couple walking hand in hand into the rental office. It made her think about Greg even more. Made her wish she had never left without him knowing the truth.

The clerk pecked away at the keyboard. She raised her head, smiling. "I found the perfect vehicle for you. It's a fire engine red twenty-fifteen Cadillac. That baby washed and ready to go!"

Naomi smiled softly. "Perfect."

Pulling onto her mother's street brought back childhood memories. Most of them were worth reminiscing over, others weren't. For what it was worth, her parents had done the best they could with what they had to raise her. Her mother had been a homemaker and her father had worked at a local grocery store as an overnight stocker, barely making minimum wage. He had taken pride in his job and worked from sunup to sundown to support his family. He even worked on holidays and birthdays, but never Christmas. It was something about the Christmas holiday that kept him home with his family, but the very next day he would be right back to work, slaving for the bare minimum. He worked the same job until he was sixty-one.

Naomi's eyes began to water. Aware that his health had become a concern, she dreaded the day she would receive that phone call from her mother in the middle of the night informing her that her father had slipped away in his sleep. The night his heart finally gave out on him, Naomi and her mother lost the first true love of their life. That was when the bottle became her lover and her best friend. When every argument and lonely grieving moment resulted in her barricading herself from the world and relying on alcohol to comfort her in a way her husband failed to. She had never owned that truth until now. Never wanted to associate her father's death with her becoming the drunk none of her family wanted anything to do with.

More emotional now than she had been that morning, she blotted the tears from her eyes. Her mother didn't need to see her for the first time in years as an emotional wreck. No, she didn't need to see her like this. It would only defeat the purpose for her being here. Her father would want her to be the strong woman he had raised her to be.

When Naomi pulled into the cul-de-sac, she recognized the vehicle in her mother's driveway instantly. "Shit! What the hell is *he* doing here?" she huffed. She slammed her foot on the brake, threw the car into park, and snatched up her $2,000 purse from the passenger seat. A furious rage overcame her. A fire fueled by nothing but resentment coursed through her small veins until suddenly, she remembered that she was not that broken, selfish alcoholic anymore who had practically traded in her family for the booze. Naomi was new and improved and she could walk in that house with her head held high because she no longer had anything to be ashamed of.

Donned in a black-and-red peekaboo fishnet top and a pair of black leather leggings, Naomi moved swiftly in her matching four-inch booties around the perimeter of her mother's manicured lawn. No matter the season, her mother had always prided herself in having the best yard on the street. Today was no exception.

She walked right up to the screen door and like many times

before, not only was it unlocked but so was the main door. Instead of knocking, Naomi walked right inside. At first glance, the place hadn't changed a bit. Everything seemed to be in the same order as she last remembered. Pictures of the entire family hung all around the three-bedroom house and as Naomi tried to make out each photo her eyes landed on, the familiar voices in the background redirected her attention. She started for the back of the house. As the muffled voices became clearer, she prepared herself. She hooked a right and the first person she laid eyes on when she walked into her mother's bedroom was her ex-husband, Charles Brooks. Her breath quickened as her eyes darted from his outdated tired ass to the slender, fashionably dressed, young woman spoon-feeding her sickly mother.

"Naomi," Charles acknowledged with unsettling confusion mapped all over his face. He was still sporting the same short natural, curly cut, and despite the mystery woman's trendy upbeat ensemble, Charles was casually dressed down in a plain gray shirt and matching jogging pants. He was about as simple and mundane as they came.

The young woman seated on the edge of her mother's bed looked up at Charles wide-eyed and then at Naomi with equal surprise. She came to her feet and placed the bowl of soup on the bedside food tray. The sudden eerie silence was discomforting. It was as though they had all seen a ghost.

"Well, what a surprise," Naomi said pointedly, followed by an inconspicuous roll of the eyes. The wavy, flowing weave hid her nice and perky breasts, but not for long. Naomi flicked her hair softly in one gesture and her brick-house body was on full display. She owned the room in that moment and made damn sure Charles took careful notice to her shapely curves and the minor cosmetic work she'd had done. Her glowing brown skin was so tight and youthful, she didn't look like she had aged at all, while unfortunately for Charles, he looked like he had time traveled into the future by twenty years. From her guesstimate, he'd gained at least thirty pounds, and his chubby face was peppered with gray hair.

Light on her feet, Naomi moved closer to her bedridden mother, stopping midstep to place her handbag on top of the dresser as though it were in an exhibition. The woman who stood shoulder to shoulder beside Charles stepped aside so that Naomi could tend to her own mother.

"We usually come by every day to check on Edna," Charles informed her. "To feed her, bathe her, make sure she's taking her meds, and to help out around the house."

"Well, that's no longer necessary. I'm here now," Naomi asserted. She ran her fingers gently over her mother's cold hands before giving her a kiss on the cheek. "I got here as fast as I could, Mama." Edna was so fragile. So weak. She was practically bones compared to the healthy plump woman Naomi remembered. The long, thick, silky hair that she had played in as a child, had thinned out, leaving numerous bald patches throughout Edna's scalp. It took everything in Naomi to fight back her tears. She had abandoned her family for so long that she hadn't realized her mother was even sick, let alone dying.

Edna took deep breaths. "We've all missed you, chile. Me, your brother, your children..." Naomi exhaled sharply, trying her best to maintain her grip on the anger and pain mounting inside of her. The man she vowed to hate for the rest of her natural life was standing two feet away from her. The man who had turned her own children and family against her. The man who had walked out on her when she needed him the most.

"What make you go off and disappear like that?" her mother questioned.

There was only one direction the conversation would turn if she opened her mouth and spilled everything off her chest. Seeing Charles and being that close to him had already stirred the resentment she'd carried around all these years. It provoked her to do ungodly things that she knew she would have to answer to later on if she dared acted on them. Deep down, part of her didn't even care. That's how much she hated that man. He deserved to experience the same pain she had, but luckily for him, now was not the time.

"We'll speak about it in private, Mama. We have a lot of catching up to do."

"That we do." Edna raised herself up more in the bed. "Until then, I need to go pay my water bill." It was her way of kindly letting them know that she needed to be excused to the bathroom.

Naomi pulled the blankets back more and helped her mother up from the bed.

"I got it from here," Edna said. "I may have cancer, but I surely *ain't* handicapped." Edna took baby steps toward the door and in the direction of the bathroom down the hall.

Charles cleared his throat, apparently sensing the big elephant in the room. Naomi raised her head and her eyes danced with the devil's. Words could not express the coldness she felt in her heart for him, but she willed herself from lunging at him and gouging his eyes out.

"Out of respect, Naomi, this is my wife—"

"Denise!" Naomi corrected, glaring evilly at him. She didn't give a damn if the woman was his new pet hamster; if she cared to know her title, she would have asked.

"I beg your pardon?"

"Naomi doesn't exist anymore. I now go by Denise."

Charles eyed her peculiarly. He looked at his wife and then back at Naomi. With furrowed brows and a condescending smirk that she wanted to knock right into the middle of next week, he slipped his hands into his pockets. "Ooookay, *Denise*. This is my wife, Jacquelyn."

Jacquelyn extended her hand. "I'm sorry we had to meet under such conditions," she said emphatically. She smiled. "Your mother is one of the sweetest women I know."

Naomi reluctantly shook the woman's hand. She quietly checked her out from head to feet, wondering exactly what it was that drew her to that cheapskate. Naomi managed a smile. She didn't have to like this woman, but she could at least be cordial toward her. After all, she hadn't done anything to her, but there was no way Naomi could rest easy if she didn't seize the opportunity to upstage her. She coolly raised her left hand and pretended to scratch an itch on her neck so that Charles and Jacquelyn could catch a close-up of the engagement ring Greg had given her. It made Jacquelyn's wedding ring look like it came out of a fast-food kids' meal.

Going against her better judgment to let sleeping dogs nap, Naomi went for the kill. "Where are my children, Charles? You haven't said one thing about them."

"*Our* children," he emphasized, "are at home."

"Well, I want to see them."

"No."

"*No?*"

"This is all so sudden, Nao… I mean, *Denise*. You don't get to be absent all this time and then just pop up when you damn well feel like it. There's an order in place—"

"Fuck that order! I want to see my babies!"

Jacquelyn nervously touched Charles on his shoulder. "Honey, I'm sure we can work something out. Besides, the kids need to see their mother."

Naomi's breathing slowly became labored as she stood there,

her piercing eyes darting back and forth between Charles and Jacquelyn.

Charles eyed his wife incredulously. "Stay out of this!"

"Those are my babies, too!" Naomi blurted.

Charles scowled at her. "Well, isn't that an unfortunate fact. How convenient for you to remember that *now* after all these years." The lines in his forehead grew more pronounced and he clenched his jaws tighter in the same habitual manner he always had. "Now if you think you can just waltz up in here and pretend you never left, you have another damn thing coming."

"Charles, please. Let's not do this in her mother's home," Jacquelyn pleaded. "The two of you can discuss this—"

Naomi didn't back down from the challenge. She was more than ready to rip him a new one. She didn't have a flashback, she had a flash-front of her ripping his big head off with her bare hands.

"Now if *you* think," she said pointedly, stabbing her index finger into thin air, "you're going to keep my kids from me any longer, you have another damn thing coming." Her words were like flaming bullets flying out of her mouth, aiming straight for his heart. "You took them from me once, and I guarantee you it won't happen again."

"I did not take them from you! You abandoned them, remember!"

"It's time for us to leave," Jacquelyn told Charles. "This is getting way out of hand and it's not the time or the place."

"You better listen to your wife if you know what's best for you." Naomi was fuming.

"Fine! This isn't worth me getting my blood pressure up, anyway!" Charles dismissed himself at once. He pushed through their invisible circle, bumping her shoulder in the process.

Naomi didn't let her tears loose until his back was completely turned.

"Where are you rushing off to so soon?" Edna asked, stopping him in the doorway.

"Sorry we can't stay as long as we usually do, Mama. I just remembered that I have a few errands to run before I take the boys to the football game tonight." He kissed Edna on both her cheeks. "Do call me if you need anything. You know I'll come running."

"Thanks, Charles. Give my grandbabies a big kiss for me."

"You got it." He walked completely out of the room without looking back.

Jacquelyn turned to Naomi. "I'm sorry, Denise. I'll talk to him. I'm sure we can arrange something." Jacquelyn reached inside her purse and jotted something on an old receipt. "This is my direct cell phone number. You can call me any time to check on them." She smiled tenderly.

Naomi's spirit was instantly lifted as she accepted the piece of paper. Why was this woman being so nice to her? "Thanks," she said softly, tears flowing down her cheeks like rain.

"You don't have to thank me. Women should stick by each other more often," Jacquelyn said, winking her left eye. She turned away to hug Edna. "I'll see you soon, Mama." She kissed her on the cheek, then made a hasty exit once the car horn blew.

Naomi slipped the piece of paper in her bra. She would put the number to use tonight. Regardless of what Charles had to say, she was going to get her babies back one way or another.

15

The class silently watched on as Sabrina showed them the proper technique to execute a pirouette. Before shifting her attention to the mirror, she locked eyes with all twelve of her dance students.

"Watch my feet first," she instructed. She positioned one foot in front of the other. She bent her knees slightly and did a classical triple spin, ending with the perfect finish. Everyone turned their heads toward the entrance when a strong round of applause came from the other side of the room. Sabrina did a double-take and both her eyes nearly popped out of their sockets.

"Ummm…" She had instantaneously lost all train of thought. "You guys go ahead and take this time out to practice your turns." The group of dancers stood eagerly to their feet. All took to their respective corners except for Deandra who ran directly over to her father. Jeff slid his lustful eyes at Sabrina and his lips cracked the sexiest smile. She brushed it off and instead, politely waved and headed straight toward Luke.

"Nice foot work!" Luke lauded.

"What are you doing here?" Sabrina quietly lit into him.

She watched Luke's eyes dance around the room before turning them strictly on Jeff and Deandra. "I came to see my wife. Is that a crime now?"

She took a deep breath, nostrils flaring. Her heart raced but her mind raced faster. What was he thinking? Was he trying to blow their cover? Did he follow Jeff here? The back of her head started to throb. She turned to check on her girls. "You're doing great! Keep it up. Alana, lift that chin up!" Out of the corner of her eye, she saw Jeff hand Deandra some money. She then remembered this was the weekend she would be with her grandmother. Before Sabrina could convince Luke to leave, out of her peripheral, she could see Jeff heading their way.

"Damn it!" she huffed under her breath. She shifted on her foot, ran her sweaty palms over her black tights, and tried not to act any different from the times when he would drop in on practice to watch Deandra or bring her weekend money.

"Don't get your panties in a wad," Luke said behind clenched teeth. "That's if you're wearing any," he simpered, looking straight ahead.

"Mr. Jackson!" Sabrina spuriously greeted. "How nice of you to drop in."

"Well, it's a nice breezy day out. I figured I'd leave the work premises and get a jog in, but then I remembered my baby needed money for the weekend."

"Daddy's little girl, that's for sure," Sabrina smiled.

Jeff chuckled. "No denying that."

Sabrina's nerves had her on edge. She cleared her throat and gave her husband the side-eye, hoping that would cue him to play nice.

Jeff turned to Luke. "How you doing, my man? I'm Jeff." He outstretched his hand and Luke gave him a firm handshake.

"I'm Luke." His eyes toyed with Sabrina's, testing her patience. "I see your daughter's enjoying my wife's class."

Sabrina was livid and about to lose her bowels. Her eyes widened in disbelief as life seemingly drained from every pore in her face. Luke had literally knocked the air out of her lungs and everything they had done up until now felt all for nothing. Jeff coughed into his fist as his eyes switched from Luke to Sabrina. Sabrina had no reason to feel ashamed. No reason feeling this bad for betraying her lover, but she did. Those feelings that she wouldn't allow to attach themselves to her and Jeff, poured down on her all at once, and for the first time ever, her heart ached for Jeff. He didn't deserve what they had done to him.

Visibly perturbed, Jeff looked back at his daughter, then at Sabrina. "Yeah, she uh…actually *loves* your wife's class. Can't seem to get enough of it." He chuckled. "Practices around the clock…all over the house." He smiled, his eyes bouncing between the two.

Luke's sharp exhale put Sabrina on defense. As intelligent as Luke was, she knew he was reading in between the lines. In that instant it was about to become love and war.

"Honey, don't you have an appointment with a client?" she interjected.

Luke drove his hands into his pockets. "No. We rescheduled that meeting, dear," he said coolly.

"If you don't mind my asking, what kind of work do you do?" Jeff questioned.

Luke's snide grin was permanently transfixed. "I'm a private investor. I buy and resell residential properties. You?"

Sabrina crossed her arms. She couldn't believe either of them right now.

"Auto sales," Jeff said shortly.

Luke nodded as he pulled his wife's gaze into his. "Now we know who to go to for that new car you've been wanting," he mockingly suggested.

Sabrina smiled sourly. This was way too uncomfortable.

"You guys can chat all you'd like, but I have a class to teach." Without giving Luke a kiss or making final eye contact with Jeff, she walked off, suddenly too sick to her stomach to resume.

16

"All right, Mr. Dupree, we'll see you next month," the receptionist said. A smile as bright as her yellow sweater lit up the entire doctor's office. She handed Leonard Dr. Cole's business card, which had his next routine checkup appointment noted on the back.

"Thanks, Tisha." Leonard waved to the other two familiar faces behind the glass. To maintain his privacy as much as possible, he preferred to be the first one in the doctor's office and the first one out. Before entering the small waiting room, he slipped his shades over his face and headed to the pharmacy next door. Normally they would have shipped his medications right to his doorstep, but when Nadine moved in four weeks ago, he opted to pick them up at the pharmacy. He didn't want to risk the chance of them arriving when he wasn't home and her opening the box and discovering his secret. He had been very careful, even kept his antiretroviral medication in old vitamin supplement containers to disguise what they really were. He felt ashamed, but it was important that he protected what was truly at stake.

Yet, as discreet as Leonard tried to be, he felt like the letters *HIV* were smeared in bold neon letters and waving like a flag across his forehead for the entire world to see. It didn't matter that he had come to terms with his illness; he still felt like he was being ridiculed by a judgmental society.

Leonard opened the door and walked straight to the back. He was greeted by the same pharmacy technician who had been working there since he'd first started his ARV treatment. "How's your day off to, Jeffrey?"

"Can't complain, Mr. Dupree. How about yourself?" he asked, rounding the prescription counter behind him.

"I'm blessed, brother." Leonard was in great spirits when he woke up with breath in his lungs this morning, but he had also just received a positive health report from his doctor that his CD4 cell count was high and his vitals were excellent. He was thankful that the medicine was still doing its job, but he knew there was a higher power looking after him. There was much to be grateful for. In fact, he felt so good he was going to let his sister know that he would be coming down for Thanksgiving. Maybe he could convince Nadine to take the trip with him. It would be the perfect opportunity to introduce her to his family. His mom would love her. He only hoped that enough time had passed for her to completely forgive what Chasity had done to him so that she could open her heart to the new woman in his life.

Jeffrey quickly thumbed over several prescription bags before coming back around and handing Leonard the one with his name on it. "Doesn't look like anything has changed," he said.

"Fortunately for me, that's a good thing." Leonard chuckled as he eased his credit card out of his wallet.

"And here's your receipt."

"Thanks, Jeffrey. I'll see you next month."

"All right, Mr. Dupree. You have a good one!"

Half an hour later, Leonard was coasting down Interstate 35 when his cell phone rang the beautiful melody he had selected especially for her.

"Good morning, my beautiful queen," he answered.

"Good morning!"

Even in his absence Leonard could see her angelic smile and feel her comforting warmth.

"Thanks for the roses and the beautiful card. They came shortly after I returned from dropping Canvas off to daycare."

"You're welcome. Sorry I'm not there to make you breakfast. I had to skip out a little early this morning. I wanted to sneak a kiss, but you were sleeping so peacefully I didn't want to disturb you." He could hear the air lift in her breath. He switched lanes and veered toward the exit for the hospital.

"You're an amazing man, Leonard."

"And you are an amazing woman." He couldn't hide the smile that had washed over his face. He hadn't been this happy in years.

"You keep spoiling me like this and I may have to tell my real estate agent that I've changed my mind about moving."

"I'll do you one better. Give me the number and I'll call her. Because baby, I'm just getting warmed up."

17

Leonard had visited Greg practically every day since the accident. His best friend was getting better by the day and things were looking up. Given all that Vivian had gone through, she was by her husband's side every step of the way. Leonard could only hope and pray that he found that special someone in Nadine. A woman like Vivian who respected and honored her vows, through thick and thin, sickness and in health. A woman who would never leave his side, no matter the hardships they faced in life. He desired a Proverbs 31 woman; a woman of virtue, loyalty, and self-respect. The kind of woman who could reciprocate the same kind of love he would freely give her.

Sadly, in this dating era, that kind of love was rare. Women were so bitter from past relationship experiences and too emotionally scarred that they no longer trusted or depended on a man for anything. Not even sex. So good men like Leonard were pushed to the wayside. It took more to get a real woman's attention, and he was one to recognize that better than any other.

He peeped at his watch before stepping off the elevator and onto Greg's floor. Balloons in hand, he was going to surprise the old man. Hopefully get him out of that room for a spell and take him down to explore the cafeteria. He would do anything to help him get his mind off his current condition.

Leonard stopped directly in front of Greg's partially open door and knocked with his knuckles a few times before entering.

"Hi! Can I help you?" a Hispanic woman mopping the floor asked.

Leonard's eyes zeroed in on the empty bed. "Yes…I'm uh…looking for Greg Adams."

The woman changing the sheets stopped what she was doing and pointed to the white board hanging on the wall. "This Mr. Hernandez's room. Mr. Adams no longer here," she replied in broken English. "Check with nurse up front."

"*Gracias*," Leonard replied.

She smiled and proceeded to her floor duty, humming and mopping to her own tune.

Leonard headed straight for the nurse's station. It was quite possible that Greg had been moved to a different floor considering his steady improvement, but he couldn't be too sure. There was only one way to find out.

"Excuse me. I'm looking for Greg Adams."

The heavyset woman behind the desk smiled wryly. "Mr. Adams was released three hours ago."

Leonard surrendered an uneasy smile. "Thanks for the update." He immediately wondered why Vivian hadn't called him to give him the good news. It didn't matter at this point. All that mattered was that Greg was out of this hospital and back home.

"Poor Mr. Adams," the woman uttered.

Leonard eyed her curiously, hesitating to question her comment.

The nurse disdainfully pursed her lips, her pupils widening by the second.

"Whatever he did to her, he sure as hell paying for it now," she tittered, shaking her head emphatically.

Leonard was taken aback. Before he could ask the woman anything more, she began pecking away at her computer.

"I'm going on break, y'all!" she hollered to her coworkers. She gave Leonard one last sympathetic look and walked off.

Headed back to the bank of elevators, Leonard pulled out his phone and pulled up Vivian's number. Once he realized he didn't have a strong enough signal, he waited until he was completely out of the hospital before trying to reach her again.

"Hello," Vivian answered on the third ring.

"Hey, this is Leonard. Is Greg with you?" He picked up his pace as he moved in the direction of his vehicle. It was so windy out he had to tighten his grip on the string around the *GET WELL SOON* balloons to prevent any from flying away. He tucked his Bible under his left arm as he dug his keys out of his pocket. There was an eerie silence before Vivian finally responded.

"No. He's not with me." She paused again before starting back up. "He wasn't receiving the proper care in that hospital, so I had him released."

"*Released!* Released where?" Leonard was completely baffled.

"He's at Legacy Garden Aging and Rehabilitation Center—"

"You put him in a nursing home!" Leonard snapped, cutting her off.

"Don't get all hysterical on me, Leonard. It's only until he's completely rehabilitated. Once he's able to walk on his own," Vivian explained phlegmatically, "I'll arrange for him to come home."

"You really should have called me on this one." He couldn't believe his ears were hearing what they were in fact hearing.

"I beg your pardon? I don't need your consent, Mr. Dupree. I'm his *wife* and medical power of attorney in case you might have forgotten. I have every right to act how I see fit. Now, if you don't mind, I have other pressing matters to tend to. As this conversation is already beginning to cause a great deal of distress."

He took a deep breath. "I'm sorry. I didn't mean to upset you. I just…cannot imagine Greg of all people…in a nursing home," he finally churned out. He shook his head. The thought alone was too depressing. Leonard knew this was not something Greg would have wanted. Hospital yes. Nursing home, hell no!

"It's fine. I understand we both want what's best for Greg, but I assure you, he's in good hands. As a matter of fact, I'll be headed that way shortly to spend some more quality time with him. Should I tell him to expect you?"

Leonard thought long and hard. Maybe he was in fact imposing on Greg's marriage and overstepping his boundaries. He hated to do it, considering how long they'd been friends, but it was time he backed off a little. If Vivian needed him for anything or wanted his involvement from here on out, she knew how to reach him.

"I'll catch up with him in the next week or so. Just send my prayers and update me on his progress if you will."

"Of course. We'll talk soon," Vivian said before disconnecting from the call.

Leonard started up the engine. He took a mighty deep breath as he sat there contemplating Greg's situation. "A nursing home," he mumbled. He couldn't make sense of it, but there was one last important errand he needed to run before heading back to his castle to be with his queen.

18

The mall wasn't as busy as Naomi had expected it would be for a Friday evening. Maybe this was a good sign. Her right leg shook uncontrollably underneath the cocktail table as she waited for Jacquelyn. She had spoken with the woman several times before today's meeting and felt a genuine vibe about her, but her showing up today would prove if she was truly a woman of her word. Charles had another thing coming if he thought she was going to sit back another damn minute and allow him to brainwash their kids like he had done all these years. Today they would know the truth and not some fabrication of the truth. Their mother was not dead. She was very much alive and she had come to take them all home.

She checked her cell phone a second time. She and Jacquelyn had agreed on five o'clock. It was ten minutes until and Naomi couldn't calm her nerves if she tried. Her eyes bounced around the food court in search of the woman. When she didn't see her, a worried look washed over her face. Panic set in. She hoped she hadn't changed her mind. Hoped Charles hadn't figured out what they were up to. The chiming of her phone pulled her out of her thoughts. It was a text message from Jacquelyn stating that she was in the parking lot and on her way up. Naomi nearly leaped off the chair. She dug inside of her purse and popped open her compact for one last look-see. Her makeup was still fresh, but the tears filling her eyes threatened to ruin it. She quickly closed the compact and tossed it back into her purse. Her stomach was turning flips; that's how nervous and anxious she was. She finally stood up, flattened the short wrinkle in her skirt with her palm, and scooped up her purse. She walked around to the side where the escalators were, her head racing and her heart pounding the entire way.

Looking past the plump pregnant woman who looked like she was carrying sextuplets, she spotted Jacquelyn. Behind her were Charles Jr., Marcus, and DeMarcus. Tears discharged from her eyes. She tried to calm her trembling hands to no avail. Her tears rounded her apple cheeks. They were tears of happiness and pain. She had missed so many moments of their lives. Moments that she could never get back. But instead of harping over a past that she could not change, she embraced the present.

"You brought them!" Naomi's lips quivered with every word as tears rushed past her lips.

Jacquelyn smiled and rubbed Naomi's shoulder. "Just as I promised I would."

Naomi's breathing became erratic as she stood face to face with her children whom she hadn't seen in years. Charles Jr. had sprouted so much they were eye to eye, shoulder to shoulder. Her twins weren't far behind their brother. At only eleven years old, they were already five feet three. It was obvious they had gotten their height from their father. She leaned in to hug each one of them, never wanting to let go.

"Let's find somewhere to sit you guys," Jacquelyn suggested.

"Yes…there's a table right over there." Naomi pointed at the empty table. They followed her lead. She shuffled chairs around to make room at the small square table which was situated in front of Ernesto's Pizzeria.

"How about I go order us a pizza?" Jacquelyn said. The boys' faces lit up. "Don't tell me…" She pointed to Charles first. "Pepperoni." Then she pointed at the twins. "Supreme, no olives, extra cheese," she said lastly, reciting their orders from memory. They nodded eagerly and she happily got up. "Anything for you, Denise?" A peculiar look swept over the boys' faces.

"No, I'm fine. Thank you."

"Okay. I'll be right back." Jacquelyn smiled as she rushed off to place their orders.

Naomi turned her attention back to her children. She could see the questions swarming in their eyes and she was ready to answer them all, the best way she knew how.

"Go ahead. Ask me whatever you want to know."

"Why'd you leave us?" Charles Jr. spat, cutting right to the chase.

"Yeah!" the twins chimed in unison.

"Daddy said you didn't want us anymore. He said you were on drugs and living in a cardboard box under the bridge," DeMarcus said.

Tears clogged her throat and the feeling that rushed over her, seemingly paralyzed her. She fought for the right words, fought to expel all those horrible things Charles had ever said about her.

"Boys, Mommy would never leave you." She paused, pulled a napkin from the dispenser and blotted her eyes with it. "A long, long, time ago, I was very sick." She sniffled but tried to keep it together. "It was so bad that I couldn't take care of myself anymore." She made eye contact with each of them. "I battled with my illness for a very long time, until I made the decision to get the help I needed."

"What kind of illness?" DeMarcus quizzed. His thick brows furrowed behind the question and he looked more like a grown man sitting there than the child he was.

"Addiction," she blatantly admitted. "But I have been sober for more than two years now. More importantly, when I was in rehab, there wasn't a day that went by that I didn't think about you guys. Thinking of you helped me get better."

Charles Jr. gave her a once-over. "Who in the heck is Denise?" he asked flatly, sounding too much like his father.

Naomi didn't respond right away. "Denise Adams is the name I go by now." Their faces scrunched in confusion. "When I turned my life around, I wanted to shed the old me completely. During that transition, I changed my name."

"I like the old name better," Marcus admitted.

"Me too," DeMarcus cosigned.

Junior nodded in agreement. They were way too young to understand what this new beginning meant for her and why shedding the old name was not only necessary to start anew, but to feel like a brand-new woman who had been given a second chance.

Before Naomi could respond, the clicking of Jacquelyn's heels brought her to pause.

"Time to eat!" Jacquelyn said. She set both trays in the center of the two tables they'd pushed together. She handed out packets of parmesan cheese, then produced a small bottle of sanitizer out of nowhere. She began passing it around the table. "Charles, have you taken your vitamin for your iron?"

"Yes, Mama," he answered Jacquelyn.

Naomi cringed from hearing her son call another woman Mama. The guilt pushing on her chest numbed her entirely. She watched as the boys dived in and she and Jacquelyn made small conversation. They hadn't known each other long, but Naomi was grateful for her. She had made this process smoother for Naomi. It would only be a matter of time before her boys were back in her life full-time.

Once they were done eating, Naomi splurged on her children like she had never before. When it was all said and done, she had spent well over $10,000 in a matter of three hours. Nothing was off-limits; money was no longer an object. She had even bought Jacquelyn a few goodies. It was her way of saying thank you.

When it was time to depart, she hugged and kissed all three boys, hating to see them leave. They had all agreed to keep their meetings a secret. It was for the best until Naomi figured out her next move.

"Denise!" Jacquelyn called after her when she turned her heels to walk away.

"Yes," Naomi said.

"I almost forgot to give you this." Jacquelyn rummaged through her purse and handed Naomi a torn-off sheet of paper. "It's the number to the guy I was telling you about. He helped my cousin win back custody of her children after a drawn-out battle with her ex. Maybe he can help you." She smiled.

Naomi's mouth fell slightly agape; she couldn't help wondering for the umpteenth time why Charles' wife was being so damn nice. She was receiving more cooperation from her than their own father. Her eyes scrolled over the name on the paper. "I will give him a call. Thanks for going through the trouble."

"No trouble at all. Like I said before, women have to stick together."

A tear clouded her right eye. Before meeting Jacquelyn, Naomi didn't have anyone in her corner to support her through this process. Now she did. She leaned in to hug her new best friend.

19

"Oh, shit! Yeah, suck that big black anaconda!" Jeff moaned. The wall became his only support as his coworker, Christie, went to town on his dick. She was on her knees giving him one of the best sloppy head jobs of his life. He needed the release, especially after what had happened earlier today with the Sabrina situation. Good thing he had good old pipe-mouth Christie to count on in his time of need. She was always available to satisfy his every desire and there to take his mind off the irrelevancies in his life.

He winced in pleasure and pain as she dug her sharp, black stiletto nails into his ass cheeks.

He finally opened his eyes and watched her in action before closing them again. Images of Christie, Sabrina, Nadine, Ménage, LaToya, Becky, Tracy, and even his ex-wife, Denise, taunted him to no end. There had been so many women he was starting to lose count.

"That's good, baby," he said weakly. When Christie didn't let up, he said it again. She slowly unraveled her juicy pink tongue, unlocked her jaws, and released him from her nice warm mouth.

Smiling, Christie came up from a perfect squat. She ditched her beige chiffon pleated blouse, hiked up her high-waisted leather skirt, and bent over far enough for him to see that she wasn't wearing any underwear. It wasn't a surprise, given the fact that every time they had one of their little office rendezvous, he had yet to find her wearing any. Tonight was no exception. Without Christie running to his aid, he would still be thinking about that coincidental encounter with Sabrina's husband. While Jeff knew Sabrina was married, he couldn't understand why he felt like *he* had been the one getting cheated on. Sabrina was no different than the other women, only she was married. She had used Jeff for emotional comfort and sex. Both in which he had obliged. But after that close call today, he was going to put an end to it before someone got hurt.

Christie sexily climbed on top of his desk and spread her pussy lips wide open.

"Is this what you've been waiting for?" She slid her fingers in and out of her slippery rapture. Her perky breasts sat beautifully on top of her chest, summoning him to indulge in yet another one of their surreptitious late-night-at-the-office quickies. On most Fridays, they were always the first to arrive to work and the last to leave. They had the perfect window of opportunity to get in a good workout.

Hard as a rock, Jeff was ready to go deep-sea fishing. He took two steps forward and eagerly wrapped his lips around her jolly titties. The heels of her shoes clinked as she enfolded her legs around his waist.

"Give it to me now." She yearned, sliding her long slender fingers under his shirt and over his ripped body.

Jeff kissed her neck and her left shoulder, stopping abruptly to avoid any further delay. He reached in his lap drawer and quickly fished out a condom. Once inside of her, he forgot all about the women who had used and abused him. In that moment, he didn't give a damn about anything but getting his nut.

Jeff did at least eighty miles an hour on the freeway to get home. He cursed the entire way, knowing he was going to hear her mouth as soon as he got there. That was if she waited. He didn't let up off the accelerator until his wheels turned onto one of the residential streets in his subdivision. The neighborhood kids always hung out past curfew on Friday nights. He honked and waved at a few of the youngsters he recognized. They waved back and picked up their skateboards to clear the way for him to pass.

Jeff pulled onto his street and when he saw her car in his driveway, he immediately began to mentally prepare himself for war. He pulled alongside her and brought his car to a slow stop. He prolonged getting out, struggling to manufacture the best lie he could. A lie that didn't sound like a lie. He took a deep breath, shut off the engine and walked around to the driver's side of her car. He recognized that pissed-off look of hers right away. It wasn't going to be easy getting out of this one.

"Sorry I'm late," he quickly announced. "You look beautiful. As always." He smiled, hoping that compliment would change the tempo.

"What's the point of having a damn cell phone if you're not going to answer it!" Nadine lit right into him. She gave him a dirty look that dismissed his apology altogether.

"Battery died," Jeff said simply, hoping to avoid an argument.

Nadine's unbelieving eyes bore into him. She shook her head. "We agreed on nine o'clock every Friday and you can't even commit to *that!*"

His eyes tore away from her and he opened the back door to get his son. He held Canvas in one arm and grabbed his bags with the other. Realizing he owed her a better explanation than the one he'd just given her, he said, "I had a blow out on the freeway in the middle of traffic. I forgot my charger this morning in a rush to drop Deandra off at school, or else I would have called you and informed you that I would be running late. I'm sorry if my forty-five-minute delay has fucked up your weekend!"

"Don't turn this around on me," she said pointedly.

"I'm not turning anything on you, but thanks for caring enough to ask how my day went!" he shot sarcastically.

Bingo! That silenced her long enough for her to end her nagging.

"I'm sorry," she said.

Jeff was proud of himself for maintaining a straight face. He'd learned how to lie from the best of them.

"Humph! It's cool. Now if you don't mind, I would like to go get out of these sweaty clothes and hop in the shower." Her eyes roamed his clothing. He knew exactly what she was doing. She was checking for tire grime, anything that corroborated his story. "You're free to join me." He winked.

She rolled her eyes upward and started the car. "On that note, I'll be back Sunday evening to pick him up."

"I have to pick up Deandra from Grace's Sunday so I can drop him off afterward."

Silence again.

"Is that a problem now?" he asked.

Nadine met his gaze. "I don't think it's a good idea."

Jeff eyed her strangely. "Wait. Now all of a sudden you have an issue with me picking him up and dropping him off? Something's not adding up!" His face scrunched and his brows furrowed. "Where exactly is my son sleeping at night, Nadine?"

She looked everywhere but at Jeff. Finally, she muttered, "We're staying with Leonard."

Jeff's face turned to hot stones and at that point, he didn't even want to look at her anymore. He walked off and she continuously called after him.

"Jeff, wait!" He heard her engine cut off. Could hear the melody of her heels rushing after him. He unlocked the door and walked inside the dark house. He flipped on the first light he came to. Traces of Sabrina's perfume lingered in the air while Christie's erotic essence covered him like a second coat of skin. He sat Canvas in his playpen and made sure he was content before heading straight for his bedroom.

Nadine followed him. "Are you going to let me explain?"

He ignored her as if she weren't even there. He snatched off his tie and shirt, disregarding her presence. He unbuckled his pants and eased them, along with his underwear, off. When he turned around, she diverted her attention.

"We can't talk like...*this*. It's inappropriate and you know it."

Jeff walked around her in complete nakedness. "I'm in my house. I can get naked anytime I please."

"What do you want from me!" she asked finally.

He stopped and turned to face her. "You know exactly what I want, Nadine."

She scrunched her face in utter bafflement. "Stop playing these damn mind games with me and tell me what it is you want!"

"I want *you!*" He took a dangerous step closer. Close enough to taste her skin, to hear every racing beat in her heart, and to restore that connection. His eyes skipped around her body. She looked amazing in that dress and all it did was tease him to the point where he wanted to rip the damn thing off and remind her of what they once shared. Remind her of what she could never fully let go of.

"I can't do this," Nadine said, rejecting him.

He held her trembling hands before placing both of them over his own heart. "You feel that?" Nadine nodded in response as tears skated down the apples of her cheeks. "I love you," Jeff declared. "That will never change."

Nadine looked him square in his chocolate brown eyes, a glimmer of hope dancing behind his uncertainties. She pulled her hands back to her sides as if coming to her senses. "Is that why there's an open condom wrapper beside your bed?" Jeff didn't bat an eye or turn around. It was apparent she had detected his latest conquest. "Is it also why my nose can't quite decipher your sweaty phero-mones over this dreadful imitation perfume you're wearing?"

Never dropping his attention, Nadine quietly chuckled and puckered her forehead as if she'd discovered all the evidence on her own. Jeff felt like he was on trial and all the implicating evi-dence had just been produced to the jury. His balls were starting to sweat from the pressure and the charges being stacked against him. He upheld his silence, aware enough to know that denying her accusations would only land them back in the same place. He was trying to make progress and peace, not piss her off and make her sound foolish, when in fact she was right about everything.

He listened intently without interrupting her, something he rarely did. His eyes begged for her forgiveness while the pulsation in his rising erection, promised to make it up to her. Very soon. She shook her head in disappointment, refusing to acknowledge the upswing of emotions that had him standing butt-ass naked in his own truth. He had been in a hurry to erase the evidence clinging to his dick like foreskin, but now, all he wanted to do was hold Nadine and beg her to wait on him. Beg her to give him more time to get his shit together.

"What do you want me to say?" he asked pleadingly.

"Nothing, Jeff. Nothing at all! Because I actually believe you when you say you had a blowout. But we both know damn well that it wasn't on a freeway."

This time Jeff pulled back, appalled.

"Why look so stupefied? Did I strike a nerve?" she snapped, her head tilted to the right.

This wasn't getting him anywhere. He walked around her and over to the dresser. He pulled out a baby-blue pair of boxers and a wife beater. He casually laid them across the bed.

"You can believe whatever you want to believe, woman. But when he breaks your heart, don't say I didn't warn you. You can't trust a man who sends you roses every day."

"Dutifully noted from the relationship expert," she chortled sarcastically. "And wait…how did we get on Leonard? This isn't about me and my man."

"All right." He bounced his head as she eyed him disdainfully, her nose prodded in the air. "You don't have to listen to me. Hell, you're right, I'm no expert," he inanely bleated. "But rest assured he's hiding something. That's why he's overcompensating. Keep in mind that you haven't even known brotherman that long and you're already playing house with him. For all you know, he could be a damn serial killer."

"Are you more concerned about him being a serial killer, or the fact that I'm fucking someone who's not *you!*" she questioned with much attitude.

That one line punched him dead in his chest, but he managed to recover from the blow. "Something don't add up about him and I'm only concerned for my son's sake. I know guys like him. For all you know, he has a wife and kids stashed somewhere in another state. All I'm saying is, do your homework on this cat before you go falling head over heels!"

She crossed her arms over her chest and shifted her weight from one foot to the other. "Wow! You really *don't* want me to be happy. I get it now. This is why you're being so difficult and showing your true colors." She mocked him in laughter. "I think my baby daddy's a cock-blocking hater!"

"What?" His entire chest began to swell as his face tightened. He couldn't believe she went there. "You better gon' somewhere with that. I'm only looking out for you and Canvas. I would never interfere with your happiness. And sure it's funny as hell now, but you know what they say," he said, flashing a knowing grin. "Laugh now…cry later." He walked off, dismissing the conversation altogether, but not without mumbling, "I'm no cock-blocking hater. You got me fucked up. If anything, you should be thanking me for looking out for your naïve ass." Nadine must have heard him as she started up all over again.

"You're just jealous and upset that I'm moving on without you! You should be happy for me!" she yelled. "I deserve a good man! And you wanna know something else…I'll take a tub of *dead* roses over a liar, cheater, and a poor excuse of a man, any damn day of the week!"

Jeff turned on the shower and allowed the water to drown out Nadine's harangue. She was right; he should have been happy that she'd found someone to love, but he wasn't. The guilt and jealousy pulling at his heartstrings wouldn't allow him to accept that she had moved on to someone new. Even if he didn't deserve her right this moment, he knew that one day, he could have learned to love her the way she needed to be loved. Had she given him a little more time, he could have restored her trust in him. He could have made a believer out of her and fought for his chance at loving her, again. But for now, all he could do was accept the hardcore fact that he'd fucked up. He would wait it out. She was worth the wait. And if this hunch he had about this new cat in her life was right, he wouldn't have to wait very long.

20

Nadine had left Jeff's house in tears tonight. She expected more coming from him. She realized now her expectations were unrealistically too high. He had done nothing but disappoint her time and time again. How was it that he could screw random women day in and day out and still expect Nadine to believe that he was a changed man? She wasn't convinced that he could ever love and treat her how she deserved to be. And now that her head was out of the clouds, she could see that he had pulled the wool over her eyes for far too long. Jeff never was and never would be the right man for her, in this life or the next. It was time she accepted that once and for all. Their time together had run its course and his actions tonight were confirmation that she was making the right decision by giving her heart completely to the new love in her life.

As she pulled into the parking lot of Chasity's, she waved to the valet attendants Ornesto and Travis. They kindly returned the gesture and stepped to the side so that she could pull into her designated space next to Leonard's Range Rover. He didn't tell her what the special occasion was; all he told her was to wear something beautiful and join him for a late dinner. She double-checked herself in the mirror. Her long curls were all pinned to the right and fell evenly over her bare shoulder. Pleased with her overall appearance, she grabbed her clutch and stepped into the night in a black Donna Morgan brocade dress that she'd picked up from Lord & Taylor. Her shoes matched perfectly and since she had lost all of her fine jewelry in the fire, she decided on a simple pair of dangling chandelier earrings to complete the look.

She moved quickly toward the restaurant. The wind was a bit choppy and the temperature had dropped since earlier. Thank goodness she didn't have to walk far. As soon as she stepped inside the building, the heat from the fireplace hugged her. She was greeted by Bianca, the maître d' of the night.

"Good evening, Bianca," Nadine replied. "Has Leonard arrived yet?"

"Yes, ma'am. He's in back. I'll show you to him."

Nadine followed Bianca toward the rear of the crowded restaurant. When she spotted Leonard, her entire face lit up. "Thank you," she told Bianca. Leonard rose to his feet and embraced her in a hug and kiss before pulling out a chair for her.

"You look absolutely stunning," Leonard complimented.

"Why thank you. You clean up well yourself." Her eyes smiled.

"All for you, baby. All for you." He stared into her eyes for a minute longer. "How was your day?" he asked.

"Lonely without you."

"I'll make it up to you." He winked his left eye and his lips carved into that sweet sexy smile she admired so much.

"How did everything go with Canvas's doctor's appointment this afternoon?"

This was why she loved him. His own father had not even cared enough to ask how his son's appointment had gone.

"Everything went great. His height and weight is still in the fifty percentile and he's doing everything he should at this stage, including getting into everything he sees." She chuckled.

"That's my boy," Leonard exclaimed with a grin.

"Well, since that's your little roll buddy, I guess now is the perfect time to tell you that he wasted red fruit juice on your favorite rug right after breaking your Chaka Khan CD."

He grabbed his chest and sunk into the chair. "Not Chaka!" He pretended to be in dire pain.

"Sorry, love. No 'Funny Valentine' tonight." She laughed. He straightened up and laughed along with her.

"That's okay. You know why?" he asked seriously.

"Why?"

"Because all that can be replaced." He leaned in and pressed his lips to hers. Just after doing so, the waiter returned with their food and drinks. "I ordered your favorite," he offered.

"I see." She marveled over the delicious honey-ginger salmon and grilled vegetables.

"Is there anything else I can get you or your lady, Mr. Dupree?" Leonard looked to Nadine.

"I'm fine," she said.

"Perfect. Enjoy your meal."

Leonard reached over the table and grabbed both her hands. As always, he prayed over their food and before letting her left hand go, he kissed it. The romantic setting reminded her of when they'd first met. It was right here. In this room. They engaged in light conversation, enjoying one another's company until a dark-skinned woman she had never seen approached their table.

"Leonard Dupree!"

Leonard acknowledged the woman and immediately stood up to give her a hug and kiss on the cheek. "Vanessa, this is my girlfriend, Nadine."

Nadine smiled and shook the woman's hand.

"I didn't mean to interrupt," Vanessa said. "I couldn't walk out of here without at least speaking and offering my condolences."

Leonard looked down, then nodded his head. "It's okay."

"How have you been since the loss?"

He cleared his throat, turned to Nadine and then back to Vanessa. "I've managed."

"Well, I can see you're moving on and that's a sign of healing," Vanessa observed.

Nadine pulled her chair back. "I'm gonna take a quick trip to the ladies room." She smiled halfheartedly at Leonard and the woman. "Nice meeting you," she said, excusing herself.

She walked quickly to the other side of the restaurant and into the ladies room. Jealousy and uncertainty managed to creep in. Nadine tried her best to ignore it but because she didn't know who the woman was, her mind began to fill in the blanks. Jeff's words taunted her. Made her question everything her heart had yet to uncover. Having put her cell phone on silent earlier, she pulled it out to see if she had any missed calls. She had one text message from Jeff.

HE WILL NEVER LOVE YOU LIKE I LOVE YOU.

"This…" She sighed and decided to let it go. Jeff's actions made it crystal clear that he didn't know where he wanted to be, and there was no way she was going to subject herself to his bullshit anymore. She deleted the message, freshened up and went back to join Leonard.

When Nadine turned the corner, she spotted Vanessa leaving.

"You're back! I thought I was going to have to come after you." Leonard quickly stood up and pulled out her chair for her.

"I'm fine, baby." She sat down as if her mind had not been troubled earlier.

"What are the odds that I would run into my ex's hairstylist tonight of all people?"

"Humph. She seemed pretty excited to see you."

Leonard poured himself another glass of red wine and took a sip. "Yeah. Hadn't seen her in a couple of years." He inhaled sharply. "Well, that's the past. This here," he waved his finger between the two of them, "is the present and the future." He stood up from the table, clinked his fork against his wine goblet, and asked everyone in the room for their attention. Nadine looked around them with unbelieving eyes.

"What are you doing?" she whispered.

Leonard pulled the table out and positioned himself directly in front of her. She had no clue as to what was getting ready to take place, but she hoped like hell that he was not about to embarrass her by asking her to dance. She painfully recalled how horrible of a dancer he was. The brotha had two left feet and no rhythm. One night he actually had the nerve to bet her that he could beat her doing the Bunny Hop. Of course she won that bet too.

Her heart began to race and the urge to pee became tougher to resist. Invisible beads of sweat skidded down the sides of her face as he calmly took her left hand and lowered himself to one knee. Her heart literally stopped and her eyes nearly fell out of her face as they zoomed in on the ring he was holding.

"Nadine Collins, since the very moment you walked into my life, I became a better man. I prayed that God would send you to me, and He not only answered my prayers, He blessed me with your son who I will proudly call my own."

Tears rushed past her cheeks as she watched him dig into his pocket and pull out a small jewelry box. With one hand, he flipped it open and pulled out the diamond ring.

"Please give me the honor of waking up to your beautiful face every day." He paused, juggling the tears in his eyes. "Please marry me."

Although the room had come to a standstill, Nadine could hear the ooohs and awwws surrounding her. She practically melted in her seat. Her quivering lips barely allowed the words to squeeze through, but they were there. They were always there.

"Yes!" she finally blurted out. "I will marry you." She smiled broadly.

"Yes? Yes!" Leonard almost couldn't contain his excitement. He eased the ring onto her left finger and they both rose to their feet. Everyone in attendance stood, clapped, shouted and even whistled their congratulations. He placed his hands on both sides of her face and kissed her gently. "I love you," he said.

Through watery eyes, "I love you, too!" Nadine replied, feeling like one of the luckiest women in the world.

21

It had been a little over two weeks since she'd heard from Jeff. Ever since that day he and Luke showed up at the studio at the same time, he hadn't returned any of her phone calls. She had even tried going by his house, but no one ever answered the door, even when his car was parked in the driveway. He had even pulled Deandra out of dance at the school and enrolled her in a private dance studio off campus. That was when she got the message loud and clear that he wanted nothing more to do with her. They were done. It was only fair that she gave him his space; after all, their affair was subject to termination the instant she got pregnant. It was bound to end this way. All Jeff did was expedite the process.

Sabrina held the pregnancy stick between her legs as she urinated. Luke watched on intently as every second passed. They both wanted another baby so badly, and if she was in fact pregnant, this would be the start of their new beginning. With their son, Avery, she didn't have any noticeable symptoms early on. She had even managed to dodge the whole morning sickness drama that most women complained about. So other than the fact that she had missed her period, a pregnancy test was the only sure way to confirm if they were indeed expecting.

"Here," she said, passing Luke the urine-saturated stick that would soon reveal if they were going to be spending the next nine months nesting and picking out the perfect name for their little one.

"How long are we supposed to wait?" Luke nervously asked.

"The instructions said to lay it on a flat surface and the results should appear within two minutes." She cleaned herself up and walked back into the bedroom. Two minutes felt like an eternity. She peeled back the curtains and allowed some light into the room. Normally on Saturday mornings, she would go for a jog around the neighborhood. She decided against it this morning, not wanting to risk running into Jeff. Being how abruptly things had ended, she wouldn't know what to say to him.

She began to pace the floor, anxious, yet worried if the results would seriously change anything.

"We did it!" Luke shouted. He rushed into the room and over to Sabrina. "You're pregnant!"

"Let me see." Sabrina's chest felt constricted as her eyes nearly crossed trying to make out the faint positive plus sign. "Oh my God," she mumbled as her hand flew to her mouth before she could get all the words out. "I'm pregnant!" Her eyes began to gloss from tears of excitement.

Luke instantly dropped to his knees, lifted her shirt and laid his head against her flat stomach. "You're having our baby!" he shouted gleefully. He planted kisses strategically around her belly button before quickly standing back on his feet. He kissed her with such intense passion like he'd never kissed her before. They made sweet love over and over again and Sabrina savored the moment. Finally, after all they'd been through, everything seemed to be falling perfectly back into place. Exactly as they had planned.

22

"Boss lady, you're back!" Belinda greeted the second Nadine walked through the double glass doors of Platinum Crest Investments. Belinda rushed over to her boss and hugged her. "We've missed you around here."

Nadine smiled warmly. "Thanks, dear. After everything that's been going on, I needed the time to regroup before I drove myself mad."

Belinda nodded as she sympathized with her. "I completely understand. Well, you know your girl has been holding down the fort while you were out."

Nadine's face lit up. "I always know I can count on you."

Belinda smiled knowingly. She finally looked down at the bags in Nadine's hands. "Let me take some of these off your hands."

"Thanks. I thought my arms were going to fall off." Nadine made a beeline for the break-room. Judging how quiet it was, the others hadn't made it in the office yet.

"What all you got in here?" Belinda placed the bags on the table as Nadine slipped off her coat and hung it up on the wall coat rack.

"Just a few snacks." Nadine pulled out an assortment of protein shake mixes, wheat grass powder, chewy snack bars, and a variety of fruits. She had worked extremely hard getting her body back to her college figure and there was no way she was going to let herself get that out of shape again. Leonard was helpful in that area as well. He was a health nut and a great motivator. He hit the gym several times a week and exercised at home every chance he got.

Belinda's face turned sour. "Looks yummy," she lied.

Nadine chuckled. "So how's everything with you?"

"Great. I plan on enrolling in a few online classes in the spring to work on that business degree I've been aiming for. It's hard as a single mother going back to school. I'm worried if I'll be able to juggle it all."

Nadine closed the refrigerator. "I bet you can do anything you put your mind to. And you never know what opportunities await you when you're done." She smiled and winked an eye.

"Thanks. I'll keep that in mind." The phone started ringing and Belinda pulled her headset over her ears and answered the call. "Good morning, Platinum Crest Investments." She paused. "No, he hasn't made it in yet, but I'll have him return the call as soon as he arrives." She paused again. "You as well. Thank you!"

"I see we've upgraded since I've been gone."

Belinda appeared baffled. "Oh…this?" she asked, pointing to the new fancy headset. "Yes, Jim bought it for me. He said to consider it an early Christmas gift."

"How sweet of Jim."

"I know, right." She spun on her heels and reached in the refrigerator for an orange juice.

"I hope you guys are hungry!" a voice boomed from behind.

"Speaking of the devil," Nadine said. Jim walked over to where the women were huddled and placed two boxes of Krispy Kreme doughnuts onto the table. He did a double-take. "Well, stranger… welcome back!" He leaned in to hug Nadine. "I almost didn't even recognize you," he said jokingly. "We've missed you around these parts."

Nadine exhaled sharply. "Thanks. It feels great to be back. I've missed you guys, too."

"Well, when you get settled and catch your breath and every-thing, I'll brief you over a few portfolios."

"Awesome."

They both looked over at Belinda who was already on her second doughnut. She held up her left hand. "Don't judge me."

"Too late," Jim said.

They all fell into laughter.

Nadine shrugged her shoulders. "Perhaps one wouldn't hurt me," she said, reaching for a strawberry jelly doughnut. When she did, Belinda nearly choked.

"Wait! Wait! Wait! Don't tell me that's what I think it is," she said with a mouthful.

"What?"

"That!" Belinda pointed to the beautiful engagement ring on Nadine's left finger.

Jim leaned in to steal a peek. "Mighty fancy there," he said.

Nadine blushed before sharing her great news. "Well…I was going to wait to share the news with the entire staff, but since you brought it up, yes, I am officially off the market. I'm getting married!" she said excitedly.

After the staff meeting, Nadine retired to her office. There was so much work to complete that she grew exhausted simply thinking about it. However, one glance at her left hand and her mind quickly became at ease. This was finally happening for her. Her Aunt Mickey had been thrilled to hear the news as well as her soror, Kelly, and her office staff. Everyone seemed genuinely happy for her, but she knew there was one person in the world who wouldn't be. He despised that she was seeing someone else and it would kill him when he found out that she was planning to marry Leonard.

It was all the reason why she'd decided not to tell Jeff. Not that she cared if he approved or not, but she refused to allow anyone to spoil her joy. After twisting her heart and taking her in circles all these years, his input was irrelevant. It was clear he knew nothing about commitment, let alone love.

As she fell into her usual routine, the time seemed to tick by fast. Before she knew it, it was lunchtime.

Belinda poked her head through the door. "I'm going to step out and grab something from Chipotle. Want me to bring you something back?"

"Chipotle sounds great! Let me see…" Nadine pulled out a sticky note and jotted down her order. "Have them put the guacamole on the side, please."

"Got it!" Belinda slipped the note in her purse. "Be back in a jiffy!"

Ten minutes later, Nadine's cell began to buzz. It was Pamela, the realtor she had hired to help her find a new place. "This is Nadine," she answered.

"Nadine, hello! This is Pamela," she said energetically. "How are you today?"

Nadine sat upright in her chair. She didn't know how she was going to tell Pamela she no longer needed her services, but she had better do it now than to waste the woman's time. "I'm great, Pamela. I've actually been meaning to call you."

"Well, good thing I beat you to it because I think I've found you the perfect house."

"You have?" Nadine inquired, halfway interested.

"Yes! I was visiting a friend the other day and I came across a *FOR SALE BY OWNER* property that I really think you'll love. Do you think you can meet me there later today around five o'clock?"

Nadine hesitated before responding. "Sure. I can meet you."

"Perfect! I'll text you the address and will see you then."

Nadine disconnected the call. When she raised her head, Leonard was standing in her door with a single lavender rose. Her heart instantly melted as she practically shot up out the chair.

"Hey you!" Nadine beamed. "I thought you'd be in court all day." She planted her lips on his and they embraced in a nice long hug before he handed her the vase with the single rose. "Thank you!" She smiled lovingly.

"Will your staff mind if I kidnap my fiancée for lunch?"

Nadine put on a sad face. "My receptionist stepped out to grab us something. Had I known you were coming, I would have waited to join you instead."

"It's all right." Leonard pouted.

"Awww...my poor baby." She kissed his lips tenderly. "I promise to make it up to you." As she was about to deepen her kiss, they jumped at the sound of two knocks.

"It's just me," Belinda said.

Nadine walked around Leonard to grab her food. "Thanks."

Leonard slowly turned around.

"Belinda, meet my loving fiancé, Leonard Dupree."

Belinda stood frozen before slowly extending her hand to Leonard's. "Nice to finally meet you," she said, her wide eyes focused on Leonard's. She cleared her throat, seemingly lost for the right words. "Nadine...has said...nothing but great things about you." Her mouth hung slightly agape.

Leonard traded glances with Nadine and then another knock came. "Nadine, may I borrow you for a minute? I have a client I would like for you to meet," Jim said.

"Absolutely! Excuse me, guys. I'll be right back."

23

L eonard waited until Nadine was completely out the door before turning his attention back to Belinda. The moment she walked through Nadine's door, he recognized her. She had worked at Dr. Cole's office a while back as a file clerk. When he asked about her after a while, the ladies in the office told him that the temp agency had relocated her.

"It's not what you're thinking," he said bluntly.

Belinda shook her head. "Out of all the Leonards in the world, I would have never guessed it was you." She inhaled deeply. "Why are you doing this to her?"

"Doing what?" he said defensively.

"Please don't play these games. Does she know?"

Leonard looked away before answering. "No."

Belinda sighed loudly. "Oh my God." She looked as if she was going to pass out.

"We're not intimate. As if that's any of your business," he said.

"Look. Nadine is a good woman…"

"Why are you telling me something I already know?" He angled his face. "I love her. I would never do anything to hurt her." Belinda shook her head as if not believing a word being said. "I'm going to tell her in my own time and I would very much appreciate it if you not interfere with that."

"She's my friend—"

"And she's *my* fiancée," he retorted, cutting her off. "The information you have on me is solely from confidential medical records. Do you realize how much jail time you could face for violating HIPAA laws and illegally sharing a patient's records?" Belinda's face seemed to harden at the idea of serving a stint in the big house. His scare tactic seemed to be working. "Look," Leonard began more peacefully. "All I'm asking is that you stay out of my personal affairs. You do that, and we won't have any problems."

Belinda shook her head, her face scrunched with disdain. "You're wrong as hell for not telling her something as serious as this." She glared at him. "I'm going to pray about this, but most importantly, I'm going to pray for Nadine. She's a good woman and the last thing that girl needs is another brother breaking her heart." She cut her eyes evilly at him before walking off.

Leonard closed his eyes and tightened his fist. It felt as though the walls were caving in on him and he was slowly losing consciousness. As much as he dreaded it, he had to tell Nadine soon. If he didn't, there was a fifty percent chance that Belinda would, despite his warning. He walked around to Nadine's desk and wrote a quick note before making a dash for the front door. If he was lucky, Belinda would keep his name out of her big mouth, and he would wait to see Nadine again tonight for what may very well be their last time together.

24

Deandra dragged her feet into the house as Jeff's scolding continued all the way from the car. He set the bags of groceries down on the kitchen counter, rounded the island and found Deandra not far behind him with her bottom lip poked out.

"Don't give me that face," he went in again. "Because if anything, I should be pulling off this belt and showing you how I am *not* going to tolerate that type of behavior at school! You were not raised that way. How dare you disrespect your teacher like that." He tried to keep his calm, but it wasn't working. He had it in him to whip her little ass from school all the way back home, but he couldn't bring himself to do it. This was so unlike Deandra. He couldn't believe his daughter had such a dirty mouth, let alone the guts to call her teacher a bitch. When he got the phone call from Mrs. Evans, he immediately left work and hurried to the school to find out what exactly had transpired. She had informed him that Deandra was "changing" and that she couldn't put a finger on what was going on with her. But Jeff knew a fine trick to get Deandra talking.

Tears marched down Deandra's face, but he refused to fall for the guilt trip she tried to take him on. He double blinked and swore he was seeing things. He leaned in closer to inspect Deandra's face more closely.

"Please tell me that's not makeup on your face?"

Deandra kept her lips locked tight. The new set of tears streaming from her eyes were followed by sniffles and a wheezing scream that had been trapped in her throat since picking her up.

"I don't allow you to wear makeup and you know that! Who did you get it from?"

Again silence.

"Little girl, do you hear me talking to you?"

Deandra only nodded her head.

Jeff's voice deepened. "I said, who…gave you…the makeup?"

Her raging tears were starting to camouflage the pink blush on her cheeks, but the black mascara was prominent as ever.

"I…stole…it," Deandra squeezed out.

"What!" Jeff was outraged. "You stole it? Stole it from where?"

Deandra's chest heaved and her lips quivered as Jeff began easing off his belt.

"If you don't start talking, this right here is going to help you out," he warned, motioning her with the belt.

Those big brown eyes of hers widened in horror. "I took it from the beauty supply store last week." More tears crowded her face as she managed to spill out the details. "I'm sorry, Daddy," she sobbed. "I won't do it again." Deandra swiped the tears with the back of her hands. That simple gesture suddenly caused her throat to open and release a shrill cry. One he had never heard before.

"That's not going to work this time. You knew when you made the decision to steal the makeup that you were not only breaking my rules, but committing a crime. Do you know you could have gone to jail?"

Deandra stared at him dumbfounded and seemingly at a loss for words.

"They could have dragged your little ass out of there and took you straight to the big house. Do you wanna know what they do to little girls like you?"

Deandra shook her head vigorously.

"Well, keep taking things that don't belong to you and find out." His eyes scanned the room. This was one moment where he truly missed Denise. He took a deep breath. He had made Deandra apologize to her teacher and principal, but that wasn't enough. They stood in quietness as he deliberated over what her punishment would be, considering how the school was lenient enough to not suspend her for the unacceptable conduct. He dreaded punishing Deandra, but if he didn't take action now, she would assume this type of behavior was acceptable.

"No cell phone for a month," Jeff said. Deandra's face nearly melted and her mouth opened in shock. "And no outdoor play or friends over. When you get in from school, you handle your school work, chores, and then you get ready for bed," he said sternly.

"Please, Daddy. I promise not to do it again," Deandra begged.

"I'm sure you won't. As a matter of fact, I guarantee you won't."

"It was just that one time." She huffed. "Why are you punishing me?"

Deandra strained every muscle in her face and pouted her pink glossed lips. Jeff had been so upset earlier that he had failed to notice the lipstick eye shadow and blush that made her look several years older. He shook his head dejectedly, getting even more upset.

"You know what, go to your room before I tack on no television," he told her.

"This isn't fair!" Deandra whined. "I miss my mommy!" she yelled to the top of her lungs as she stormed off to her room in a tantrum. *Bam!*

"You slam another damn door in this house and I'll give you a one-way ticket to go visit her!" he yelled back. He sat there for a moment, trying to figure out where he went wrong with Deandra. This type of behavior was so abnormal for her. He remained in deep thought. The only person he would have felt comfortable in discussing Deandra with was her godmother, Nadine. She had been there for Deandra since birth and had taken on a special role in her life, but since their affair, her and Deandra's relationship had become strained. They barely spoke to one another and Jeff knew he was the only one to blame.

As he took to the kitchen to put up the groceries, his cell phone chimed. He forgot that he had lowered the volume during the conference with Deandra's teacher and principal. He picked up the phone and to his surprise, it was a text message from LaToya asking if he wanted to come over and check out her new bedsheets. He thought briefly about how he could get into a little fun with her, but before he could regale the thought any further, he reluctantly declined the offer. He had more important matters to deal with. There was definitely something going on with his baby girl and he was going to take out the time to find out exactly what it was.

25

Hell must have frozen over, Nadine thought as she pulled into the subdivision her son's father lived in. Once she made the exit off the freeway, she had begun to hatch a plan in her mind that required her to call Pamela and tell her that she had been held up at work. It would have been a lie, but the truth was, she didn't want to live in the same vicinity as Jeff, and the fact that she had driven this far for nothing was upsetting. She ditched the idea to call Pamela after remembering that she had asked Belinda to inform Pamela that she was already en route. It was too late to turn back now.

"Of all places," she muttered in disgust. It was seven minutes until five and a strong possibility that Jeff was still at work. She had no intentions of bumping into him.

She slowly pulled into the driveway next to Pamela's Camry. The curbside view was beautiful, just as Pamela had mentioned in the text, but there was absolutely no way she was uprooting to be next to Jeff.

Nadine grabbed her purse from the passenger's seat and got out of the car. Her mind had been made up several miles ago, but out of respect for Pamela's time and effort, she would at least allow her to show her around the place. Her heels clacked against the asphalt leading up to the *WELCOME* doormat. Along the way, she couldn't help but notice the *FOR SALE BY OWNER* sign perfectly positioned on the lawn in bold red letters.

She rang the doorbell once and seconds later, the door swung open.

"My sweet Nadine has arrived!" her garrulous agent sang out. Nadine forced a smile as the short blonde woman reached in to hug her. "Ooohhh…I cannot wait for you to see inside this fabulous home!" Pamela couldn't contain her excitement. "Follow me, dear," she said, leading the way.

Nadine immediately fell in love with the house the farther she walked inside. It was in impeccable shape as far as she could see. The ambiance was so inviting and the Victorian décor and artwork was richly tasteful, but there was still no way she was even halfway interested in living in the same ZIP code as Jeff. There was nothing that could deter her mind from that. Not even if the house was free.

Perusing the room for mere decorating ideas, the clacking of heels against polished hardwood wheedled her attention. She had been mistaken. She and Pamela were not alone as she had assumed. The woman moved with confidence and purpose across the room. The closer she got to where Nadine and Pamela were standing, the easier it became for Nadine to recognize who she was. It was the same woman she had met at Jeff's house that night. The woman who Jeff had claimed to be Deandra's dance teacher. Nadine's face tightened, but her transfixed stare never wavered.

"How pleasantly surprising to see you again," Sabrina spoke first. Her smile looked more like a crooked grin. It might have been a surprise, Nadine thought, but there wasn't a damn thing pleasant about it. Sabrina could not have been any more excited to see her than she was to see her. Although she didn't really know the woman well enough to judge her, the vibe she gave off was unmistakable. She extended a manicured hand to Nadine. "Welcome to my humble abode."

Nadine managed a smile in return. "I must say you have a beautiful home…Regina, isn't it?" Nadine retorted.

Pamela's big blue eyes curiously darted from one woman to the other, her Botox eyebrows elevated and an uneven smile temporarily quieted her.

"Ha, ha, ha. It's Sabrina actually," Sabrina corrected. "But I will answer to whatever name that'll help sell this house."

I'm sure you would, Nadine thought, all while maintaining her smile.

"Well, this should be easy. I didn't realize the two of you knew each other," Pamela interjected. Both women only smiled, each of their eyes sparked with impalpable distrust.

"I made her acquaintance through a mutual friend," Sabrina volunteered, her head tilted perfectly to expose the red passion marks scattered over the left side of her neck.

Nadine willed herself to not react in the manner she knew Sabrina had hoped she would and instead turned to Pamela. "I'm ready to get started when you are." Although she managed a friendly smile, it was evident her patience had been cut short.

"Why certainly," Pamela replied, quick on her feet. "Let's start in here."

Nadine followed her realtor through the house, Sabrina trailing right behind them. After a thorough tour of the property, Pamela gave Nadine a knowing look. Little did she know, there was no way in hell Nadine was buying this house.

"Ms. Montgomery, thank you for your generosity," Pamela said. "We shall be in touch."

"The pleasure's all mine." Sabrina led them through the hall leading to the front door. As she opened it, a woman with an infant strapped snugly to her bosom in a blue baby-wrap carrier came rushing across the yard. "Guadalupe," Sabrina acknowledged.

"I hope I am not too late!" the woman desperately exclaimed, clearly out of breath.

Nadine looked on wide-eyed as she and Pamela walked slightly past Sabrina.

"My husband was able to borrow the money for the down payment from his brother," Guadalupe informed Sabrina, her Spanish accent weighing heavy on her tongue. She whipped out a certified check and handed it to Sabrina. "It's the thirty-five thousand in earnest money you asked for!" she said excitedly. Her baby began to squirm and make babbling sounds that shifted everyone's attention. Never taking her eyes off Sabrina, Guadalupe began to rock in a forward motion to soothe him while instinctively slipping one hand inside the carrier to insert his pacifier.

Sabrina's eyes and lips lifted in a smile as they met Pamela's and Nadine's. "I'm sorry, ladies," she informed. "But this property is no longer for sale."

Guadalupe turned to the women wearing a smile that could stretch around the equator. She looked as though she had just been granted her dying wish. Nadine was unfazed, but she couldn't say the same for Pamela who had immediately sunk into the sulks. They both watched on as the woman raced to remove the *FOR SALE BY OWNER* sign out of the yard.

"My first home!" she yelled, practically dancing with the red-and-white sign.

It was all for the better, Nadine thought, feeling a sense of relief that she wasn't the one having to disappoint Pamela.

"I'm so sorry about this, Nadine."

"Please, don't be." They looked at the dancing woman again. "I guess it was meant to be." She sheepishly smiled.

26

His mind swarming with worry, Leonard tried his best to tune out the madness. To walk in his truth meant accepting that he was HIV positive and unfortunately one of the unluckiest faithful men alive. He hadn't done anything to deserve this, but who said life was fair. Time was not on his side and today had proven to be the perfect reminder. Seeing Belinda at Platinum Crest had forced him to lay down his burdens and accept the inevitable, as painful as it would be. It was time Nadine knew this very private secret he had been keeping from her.

As he prepared dinner and entertained Canvas simultaneously, he quietly prayed for Nadine's understanding and unwavering love and support. Hopefully God was listening.

27

Nadine's precious tootsies were killing her. The heels of her feet felt like she'd been walking on molten rock and with every additional step she took, the pain intensified. She had been away from the office for so long she'd forgotten what walking around in a pair of new high-heels that hadn't quite been broken in, actually felt like. Not to mention she had to endure the extra drive across town to meet with Pamela which added an excruciating two-hour delay to her normal arrival time. She was still peeved about that. The drive had turned out to be a waste of gas, a waste of mileage, and a waste of time. All she wanted to do now was wind down from a long hectic day.

She tottered across the parking lot, headed straight for Leonard's loft. Once she reached the sidewalk, she quickly stepped out of her shoes and walked barefooted the rest of the way. She couldn't make it to Leonard's door fast enough.

Nadine could hear sweet jazz pouring from the other side of the door as she approached it. That inviting melody brought a knowing smile to her face, but it was the urgency to see her two favorite men and the aromas seeping through the cracks that had her whipping out the shiny gold door key. She twisted the door-knob and bore witness to a picture-perfect Kodak moment. Her smile lifted as she watched the man of her dreams and the love of her life. Leonard was setting the table and singing and dancing with her son clamped to his hip. He sounded real good, too, from where she was standing and he moved like a smooth operator.

Dressed down in a plain white T-shirt and blue jersey shorts, he still turned her on. Her eyes roved his shiny bald head and lanky, chocolate, incredibly fit body. Her thirsty pussy began to throb as she imagined his full chocolate lips tickling the skin between her thighs. Her feelings were dangerously entangled, but that's what made their relationship so unique. She didn't have to spend years getting to know Leonard when her heart, body, and soul reassured her that he was the one. Many nights alone in that bed, she secretly imagined what their first time would feel like. Would the sex be the greatest she ever had? Was his sexual stamina as high as hers, and did he prefer his final lovemaking round to be rough, soft, fast, or slow? Was he a two-minute man or could he go for hours, even days. All those questions, right along with the infamous magic number he was packing, swarmed around in her head. She was sexually starved and despite the celibacy vow she'd made, she had also refrained from masturbation. No sexual release whatsoever had amounted to a very stressed-out kitty, and Nadine was paying for it. The temptation was so strong, she could barely function without thinking about sex. She had even begun to wonder if that sexual pledge had been a mistake. Jeff Jackson was one thing, but a man as fine and loving as Leonard didn't deserve to be deprived, and tonight, she was going to turn things around in both of their favor.

She quietly eased the door shut, not wanting to interrupt this beautiful moment. When Leonard finally looked up and saw her standing there, he grabbed the remote off the bar and lowered the volume. She smiled and dropped her shoes to the floor.

"My beautiful bride-to-be is here," he said, rushing over to her. He cradled her face and kissed her lips. "Softer than cotton, sweeter than candy." He smiled. It was *that* look that made her feel like she was the only woman in the world. *That* look that made her want to put Canvas to bed so that she could make beautiful, passionate love to her future husband until the moon cried.

She pushed her horny thoughts to the side and peeled off her blazer. Leonard took it along with her purse out of her hand and hung them both on the coat rack.

"How was your day, baby?" he asked.

She released a deep sigh. "Interesting," she summed up. She puckered her lips and leaned in to kiss her smiling son who had gotten quite comfortable with his stepfather.

"Well, I'm ready to hear all about it," Leonard said.

Nadine smiled at him so lovingly. "I'm going to go slip into something more comfortable. And then, I'm all yours."

Not even ten minutes later, Nadine rejoined them downstairs. Leonard placed Canvas in his new highchair, grabbed her by the hand, and led her right over to the candlelit dinner table. Like the gentlemen he was, he pulled out a chair for her, kissing her again.

"I couldn't resist," he said before heading back into the kitchen. He returned with two plates. "Our son has already eaten. It's Mommy's turn," Leonard said, placing a plate before her. He proceeded to dim the lights, creating the perfect ambiance.

Nadine looked over at Canvas and back at Leonard. "Smells delicious," she said, hungrily eyeing the plate. Cooking was one of Leonard's many talents and that was a good thing because Nadine was no Aunt Jemima or Gina Neely. If it required more than a simple push of a microwave button or didn't already come pre-prepared for the oven, it was not on her menu. She barely knew how to boil water, let alone cook a five-course meal.

"Hope you like it," he said. "I added a little twist to it. It's pan roasted lemon fish with ginger pea risotto."

"Yummy. My mouth is watering," she said, ready to dive right in. He poured them both a glass of wine before taking his seat across from her. He reached for her hands. Following his lead, she bowed her head as he blessed their food.

After dinner and pouring out the ruckus of the latter part of her day to him, Leonard volunteered to bathe Canvas while she soaked in a long, hot bubble bath. Fifteen minutes into her nightly ritual, he walked through the door. It was the first time he had ever ventured outside of his comfort zone.

"Canvas is fast asleep," he reported with a smile, passing Nadine a second glass of red wine.

She shifted in the water. "The little rascal is already out." She took a seductive sip from her glass. "You're that good, huh?"

Leonard nodded his head confidently. "That good, baby."

She lowered her eyes and brought the glass back to her lips. Was it his intention to get her drunk? She smiled as she placed the glass beside the tub. Little did he know, she didn't need alcohol to get her fire roaring. She was willing and more than ready to turn things up a notch. She sat up further in the tub, allowing the sudsy bubbles to glide down her breasts.

"I wonder what else you're good at," she said, a seductive smile playing behind her words. If she wasn't mistaken, she swore she saw the crotch of his pants acknowledge her curiosity. That was a good sign. By the time the bubbles completely vanished from her upper body, she was baring it all. Her round chocolate nipples stood erect and desperate for his attention.

Leonard peeled off his shirt, revealing a mountain of hard work and dedication. As her eyes danced in delight, she hoped this was the moment she had been waiting for. She bit down on her bottom lip in anticipation of his next move.

Leonard grabbed a bottle of vanilla-scented bath oil off the counter. He walked to the foot of the tub, eased to the floor and reached inside the water for her right leg. He kissed her ankle and aching heel before commencing to suck every toe. She moaned in sheer delight at how good it felt to have a man catering to her needs, but what would really make her night was him picking her up and carrying her back into his room. There was much to be discovered and she was ready to explore the other side with him.

Nadine's head fell back. She closed her eyes and relished in the moment. Next, she felt Leonard pouring warm oil over her legs. Using his manly hands, he worked it into her skin before proceeding to massage every inch of her feet.

When she finally opened her eyes again, Leonard was staring at her. It was as if he was studying every beauty mark on her illuminated body.

"I love you so much," he said.

"I love you, too," she replied. "In fact, I love you so much, I'm hoping we can make tonight extra special." She felt his eyes slowly pull away. "What's wrong?"

"Baby, we don't have to rush into this."

"And we're not rushing into anything." She collected her thoughts. "I feel like enough time has passed. To hell with the vow. I want to feel you inside of me."

The look in his eyes and the shift in movement told her she wasn't going to get her way tonight. She remembered the saying, *Be careful what you wish for*, and boy, was she the one getting the short end of the stick. In actuality, her celibacy vow had been nothing more than a pussy tantrum to get back at Jeff. Now, it was seriously interfering with her having her sexual needs met. She cursed the author who had written the article which had inspired her to make the overzealous commitment.

"Nadine, I want you, too. You have no idea what it would mean to me to give you every ounce of my love…but…"

"But?" Her brows furrowed in confusion and her pussy walls practically collapsed in disappointment. A night of blissful sweaty passionate lovemaking had just gone out the window. What was so hard about this? They were both in love and they were engaged to be married. Why couldn't she test out the equipment beforehand? Why couldn't he be like all the other men who could not have given a damn about some sexual pledge, and fuck her! One night of orgasmic bliss was all she was asking for.

Leonard took a deep breath. As that suffocating moment of truth hung in the air, Nadine began to feel uneasy.

"I want our first time to be amazingly special," he explained. "Memorable. Sentimental." He reached for her hand and kissed her fingertips. "I want the day that you welcome me inside of you to feel like a major event that we've never attended before. More like a once-in-a-lifetime experience that connects us on the deepest level a woman and man could ever bond on. And when that day happens, and you better believe I'm building up for it"—he chuckled—"I prefer it be on the night I officially make you my wife."

Tears began to well in her eyes. All that did was ignite an even hotter fire between her legs. She was still disappointed, but she understood how very special he wanted their first time together to be.

"Well, you know what. I don't want or need a wedding. Let's do it! Why wait when it's something we both want," she said adamantly. "I am ready to turn the page and start the next chapter of our lives together *now*."

Leonard stared at her wide-eyed. "How…soon…is…*now?*" he asked more carefully.

"Next month. We can elope. Go to Vegas. Find a chapel. There's nothing holding us back from doing this." She smiled as she con-jectured how many days she had before she could experience this event he spoke of.

"Are you sure you're ready to do this? There's time to really think this through."

She crawled down to the end of the tub, splashing him slightly during the shift. She cradled his soft chocolate face in her slippery hands.

"I am more than ready to become Mrs. Nadine Dupree." She planted her lips against his and they fell into a deep, passionate kiss. As much as she hated it, he was definitely worth waiting for. A few more weeks wasn't going to put her pussy out of commission.

"Come on, let me get you out of this tub." He stood up and reached in to pick her up, obviously unafraid to get a little wet. His hands pressed against her wet ass was torturous in itself, but Nadine fought off the compulsion. He grabbed the body oil and towel she had laid out and carried her into his darkened sanctuary and over to his king-sized bed. R&B slow jams played softly in the background, predicting the mood, yet respecting their boundaries. Leonard laid the towel down first before placing her in the center of it. A delicious harmony of two lustful beings, one completely naked, willing and able, coupled with the perfect opportunity, rested in that moment. Nadine's legs slowly began to drift apart as the urge returned with a vengeance.

Leonard leaned in, brushing his lips over her neck and lips. She quivered underneath him, nearly cumming from the unsexual tempo drumming between her horny thighs. He picked up the bottle of oil, poured it over her belly, and worked his hands all over her body. He had the unending patience of Job, and the self-control he was endowed with indicated to Nadine that not all men operated in the same fashion, as she had once believed. He was nothing like Jeff, the man that she had spent hours, days, weeks and years getting to know, only to not know him at all. Leonard appreciated and respected her. He valued her worth, and no man had ever treasured her in that way. He was perfect for her and if she didn't know it then, she knew it now.

28

"What day is it, Naomi?" her mother asked as she sipped from her glass of water.

Naomi lifted her head from the magazine she had been reading. "It's Tuesday, Mama." She didn't correct her mother for calling her Naomi. She figured it would be pointless to keep doing it, seeing how she refused to accept her new name.

"Tuesday, already?"

"Yes, ma'am."

"Well, that means my nurse is coming to visit."

"Oh shoot. Yes! She called earlier this morning while you were asleep and said she will be running a little late. She had a car accident dropping off her daughter this morning."

Her mother's left hand flew to her chest and the wig Naomi had bought her nearly flew off as she whipped her head in Naomi's direction. "Oh Lord. I hope everyone is all right."

Naomi smiled at her mother which she had dressed in the new purple silk gown she'd bought for her. "She sounded fine so I'm sure they were all okay." She paused. "Speaking of being okay, how are you feeling?"

Her mother let out a sharp exhale. "Better than yesterday and better than the day before that."

"Good. That's what I was hoping to hear," Naomi said, smiling. Suddenly the doorbell rang. "I bet that's Judy." Naomi got up and walked to the front of the house. She opened the door. "Good morning," Naomi greeted, allowing her inside. Naomi immediately thought the woman looked way too young to be experienced or even qualified to care after her ill mother. She would make a point to check into that. Naomi felt her mother deserved the best care and treatment money could procure, and seeing how she had this hand-me-down nurse coming to check on her, it was evident the state didn't feel the same way. Suddenly the nurse's age was no longer a factor; after today her mother would have an entire dream team of nurses catering to her, no matter the cost.

"It's a bit nasty out there this morning," Judy said. "I apologize again for running behind schedule. With the accident and the rain…"

"Don't worry; she's been in great hands. I'm her daughter, Denise."

The white pale-faced woman had a puzzled look on her face. "Ooooh. I don't recall her mentioning she had *two* daughters."

Naomi shook her head. "Humph. Pardon me. It's *formerly* Naomi, but I now go by Denise."

Judy's expression changed quickly. "Awww…that explains it," she said with a couple of nods of the head. She looked around the living room, taking obvious notice to the new furniture and interior decorating Naomi had done. During her short time there, she had already transformed the place and had planned to do so much more.

"Where should I sit my things?"

"Anywhere you'd like," Naomi said. "Mother's in the back. I'll be out of your way, but if you need me for anything I'll be right here."

"Perfect!" Judy set her purse and bag down on the leather sofa. She opened the bag and pulled out a stethoscope, blood pressure monitor and green folder. She zipped the bag and headed toward the back.

Naomi headed for the guest room to retrieve her purse. She had some important phone calls to make this morning. The first one was to the attorney Jacquelyn had told her all about. She really hoped he could help her get her kids back. Locating the strip of paper with the number on it, she quickly whipped out her cell phone and began to dial. The phone rang four times and Naomi worried she wouldn't be able to reach him. Right when she was prepared to hang up, his voice boomed through the line, slightly catching her off guard.

"This is Leonard Dupree."

"Hello, yes. My name is Denise. I was referred to you by a friend who knew someone that you represented in a custody case. She said you might be able to help me."

"Thanks for calling, Denise. I would love to hear more, but unfortunately, I'm booked until the middle of next month."

"The middle of next month?" Naomi wanted to be sure she'd heard him right.

"Yes, ma'am. If you're needing someone to look into your case sooner, I can recommend a good friend of mine."

"No…no. That's okay. I'm sure your friend is great; it's that I…" She exhaled, getting more frustrated. Unannounced tears jetted down her face. "I'm sorry," she began again, her words splitting in half along the way. "This is really difficult for me."

"I understand."

"I can pay you double your fee," she blurted out in a desperate attempt.

Leonard cleared his throat. "Double?" he questioned as if he was seriously giving it some thought.

"Yes! Double."

Silence.

"You know, Ms. …"

"Mrs. Adams," she interjected.

"Mrs. Adams," he stated as if he were making a mental note.

There was a brief pause on his end. "How about we start with a phone consultation, let's say, Thursday at nine o'clock."

She was finally able to breathe again. "That sounds good to me."

"Great. I'll lock in this number you're calling me from and we'll speak then."

"Thank you!" she said before ending the call. She sighed in relief. If Leonard could help her, there was a good chance she could have her kids back in no time. More tears welled in her eyes. Her children meant the world to her and there was no way she was going to sit back and do nothing. They belonged with her. She was their mother.

After programming Leonard's number into her phone, Naomi continued to make her next call. She had received the email from her attorney's assistant that her new driver's license and social security card were waiting for her at their office. She had asked that they hold them until she returned to L.A. but figured what was the point in waiting. Instead, she was going to have them rush the docs to her mother's house. After having to endure so many changes and setbacks, this was one life-changing decision that she could not be more proud of. The name Denise fit her so well, too. As she came into this new version of herself, she simply felt as though she'd been born again. It didn't bother her that she had assumed the identity of a dead woman—Greg's former lover to be exact. Becoming Denise meant starting anew and shedding a past she had been trapped in for years. Besides her children, she wanted to rid herself of everything that reminded her of Naomi Brooks, and seeing her picture beside her new name would complete the transformation. All her heart longed for now was for her mother to make a miraculous recovery, to gain full custody of her children, and to be reunited with her love, Greg. Only then would she be complete.

29

He had felt good about today's hearing and his clairvoyance had been spot-on, again. With God's favor and Leonard's devotion, another father was happily united with his four children, despite his ex-wife's wishes and failed attempts. Though he paid his child support faithfully, she had kept his children from him for two years out of pure bitterness. Judges were always able to see through those types of cases, and it was crystal clear that the father had done everything in his power to maintain stability. He had even proven that he could support his children without any help. It was a hard-fought battle, but Leonard liked to believe that everything happened for a reason.

While the majority of his clients were women, Leonard also represented a great deal of men who had been wrongfully accused of being deadbeat fathers when in fact it was the opposite. In many scenarios, his male clients had avaricious baby mamas who expected their lofty lifestyles to be supported in addition to the children. When that didn't happen, innocent children were used as pawns and the father either lost custody or were withheld visitation rights without proper reasoning. Today's case had undergone the same vigorous process, but luckily for him, Malik had followed every bit of Leonard's advice.

Leonard headed out of the George Allen court building dressed in one of his favorite gray tailor-made suits and a matching tie;

briefcase in one hand and an umbrella in the other. The weather had gotten much nastier than it had been early that morning. Good thing he remembered to close the sunroof. He hurried down the eight steps and walked even faster to his car, trying not to get his suit touched by the rain.

"Wheww," he exclaimed, opening the door of his car and climbing inside. The fresh leather smell was as potent as ever after recently having his car detailed. He placed everything in the backseat and started the engine. Normally right after court, if he didn't have errands to run or significant business to tend to, he would swing by the restaurant to help out, accept that phone call he received earlier from Mrs. Adams had put something else on his mind. It was about time he went to go check on his friend.

To his surprise and concern, he hadn't heard one word from Vivian since their last disagreement about her putting Greg in a nursing home, or as she put it, "*a rehabilitation center,*" and it bothered him. Perhaps she was still upset with him for expressing his difference of opinion on the matter. He would have preferred Greg be sent to a private hospital or facility that specialized in physical therapy services as opposed to a nursing home. It wasn't like they didn't have the money to afford the care.

Never wanting a disagreement to cause a rift in his and Vivian's friendship, he didn't press the issue. Even stayed behind the scenes, but he thought surely she would have called by now and given him some kind of update.

Thankful for his reliable memory, Leonard programmed the name and address of the facility where Greg was being treated into his GPS. He drove below the speed limit to the other side of town. He had a lot to think about during the forty-five-minute drive, including his conversation with his fiancée the night before. Whether she was seriously ready to get married or not was no longer in question. However, his concern was how quickly she wanted to make that leap. There was no doubt in his mind that she was the woman he wanted to spend the rest of his life with, nonetheless, he still had not come clean with her about his health. Guilt plagued him all night and he tossed and turned, worrying about how she would react. The longer he prolonged telling Nadine, the harder it would be for her to forgive him for not being upfront with her.

Exactly forty-two minutes later, he pulled into the parking lot of Legacy Garden Aging & Rehabilitation Center. He reached for his umbrella, got out of the car, and started for the brown brick building. An elderly man and woman in wheelchairs politely greeted him when he walked through the sliding glass doors. What caught his attention immediately was all the colorful flowers and greenery everywhere he turned his eyes. It even smelled like gardenia and rose, pleasantly alluring. A fair-skinned, slender woman with earrings that looked more like bracelets was giving room directions to the hard-of-hearing woman in front of him. She had to repeat herself at least six times before the woman finally nodded and walked off. He stepped up and took immediate notice of the clerk's nametag.

"How are you doing today, sir?"

"I'm fine, Teresa. And yourself?"

"Can't complain," she said, smiling.

Leonard flashed a smile that exposed his pearly whites. "I'm here to visit Mr. Greg Adams."

"All right. If I can get you to sign in right here," she said, pointing to a blank spot on the clipboard with her long French tip polished nail.

Leonard picked up the pen and began filling out the visitation sheet. He stopped when he came to the room number line.

"Could you happen to provide me with his room number? This is my first visit."

"Absolutely!" She began pecking away at her keyboard. Mr. Adams is on the third floor in the rehabilitation unit. Room three seventy-five," she continued. "If you take the blue elevators to the left, it'll place you at the end of his hall."

"Thank you." He wrote the room number on the paper and jotted down the time. She handed him a visitor badge which he pinned to his tie.

Taking off for the bank of elevators he couldn't help but notice how friendly everyone was. Several women greeted him in passing with smiles or a simple hello. Four of them worked there and the other three appeared to be residents.

When he came to the third floor, he headed down the hall in search of room 375. When he finally reached his destination, he took a deep breath, unsure of what condition his friend might be in behind that door. He said a quick prayer before walking in.

"Looks like you have a visitor, Mr. Adams," the aide attending to him said in her country Texan accent.

Leonard walked farther into the room. "How you doing," he spoke to the nurse. He turned to Greg. "How you doing there, buddy?"

Greg stared at him as though he had never seen Leonard a day in his natural-born life. A look of confusion swirled in his eyes as he lay there motionless. The aide lowered the volume on the television so they wouldn't have to compete.

"Can you say something for your friend here?" she asked Greg.

Greg continued to lie stiffly in silence. Leonard could barely withstand the sight of his only friend in this type of condition. It pained him to see him lying there in such a state of destitution. He sighed deeply as he turned his head and looked around the spacious room. There were teddy bears and get-well balloons all over, but what really put a smile on his face was the knitted blanket at the foot of Greg's bed. It was blue, brown and ivory with several pictures of Greg and Vivian. His eyes switched to the small bedside table where a wedding portrait of he and Vivian sat.

"How's he doing?" Leonard finally asked the aide.

She crossed her arms and peered at Greg. "Not much of a talker, I can tell you that." She tittered. "He seems to be showing minimal improvement with his physical therapy sessions, but as time passes, we're hopeful things will turn around completely. He's definitely a fighter; there's no doubt about it." She smiled. "I believe he'll come out of this stronger than ever. Ain't that right, Mr. Adams?"

"I believe that he will, too," Leonard concurred.

Beaming, the aide grabbed her clipboard and walked around the bed. "I'll be back to check on you, okay?"

Greg blinked his eyes and let out a slow and weak, "Okaaay."

"That's my boy!" she said. She turned back to Leonard. "Nice meeting you, Mr. ..."

"Just call me Leonard."

"Got it. Well, I'm going to leave you two alone. I'll be up front if you need anything."

"Thanks, Dori," Leonard said, catching her nametag. She blushed as she walked past him.

He waited until the door closed completely before he took a seat in the green chair across from Greg's bed. "Is it me, bro, or is it hot as hell up in here?" As he began removing his jacket, he saw the quilt move out of the corner of his eye. He looked up and Greg was sliding his legs off the bed. "Whoa, whoa, whoa, what are you doing?"

"Get...ting the fuck...up...out of...here," Greg slurred. He struggled to his feet as Leonard watched in disbelief and confusion. "That...bitch...tried to *kill*...me!"

"Who, Dori?"

"No. My...*wife!*"

30

In only two days, Sabrina managed to scam three homebuyers out of earnest money for a house that they would never own. She and Luke had until midnight to quietly vacate Ms. Rester's house without anyone noticing or raising suspicion. They had discussed leaving town and moving in with Luke's brother in Wyoming until things cooled off. Had even planned out how they would use the money as a fresh start to get on their feet and prepare for their new arrival. But last night something happened. Sabrina started bleeding. Badly. She knew exactly what had happened and while it hurt her to lose another baby, this time it really wasn't meant to be. It would devastate Luke if he knew what happened, which is why she decided not to tell him this soon.

Gifted with the power of persuasion and the face of an angel, Sabrina could convince anyone of anything. She had learned from the best teacher—her mother. Yet, she still couldn't fully comprehend how anyone could be so naïve. She hated that she had resorted to this type of human being. Had promised herself she would never be like her manipulative and conniving mother, but as she totaled the amount on the deposit slip and walked it over to the cashier, she realized the apple didn't fall far from the tree. It was exactly whom she had become.

"Good morning, Mrs. Montgomery. What can I do for you today?"

"Good morning, Ruby." Sabrina placed the three cashier's checks on the counter and slid them over to the gray-haired woman. "I would like to deposit these in my joint checking account."

"Okay. I'll be happy to take care of that for you," Ruby said, picking up the checks and deposit slip. She slipped on the glasses that hung from her neck.

"There won't be a hold on these, will there?"

Ruby examined the checks one by one. "I'll tell you what, for you, I'll waive the hold." She smiled.

Sabrina patted the brown faux fur scarf around her neck and smiled. "How kind of you. Mr. Montgomery and I have always been fond of the exceptional service here."

"Well, it is our job to keep our customers happy." Ruby validated Sabrina's receipt for the $105,000 and handed it to her. "Here you go. It will be available to you first thing in the morning. Did you have any plans for it?"

The question caught Sabrina off guard. "Not necessarily," she replied.

"Well, we do have a few interest-bearing products that you may want to consider. In the meantime, here's a brochure. I can have one of our bankers call you if you'd like."

Sabrina cleared her throat. She knew the money would be gone in no time. Her plans were to wire the money into an untraceable account as soon as the funds were available.

"How about I give them a call next week. I'm leaving town tomorrow and won't be back until then."

"Oh wow. Where are you going?" Ruby inquired.

Nosey old bitch, Sabrina thought. "Manhattan," she lied. "I have some family I'm going to visit."

"How nice. Well, have a safe trip going and a safe trip coming back."

"Thank you." Sabrina quickly stepped out of line before Ruby could pry any further. She placed her shades back over her eyes and sauntered through the lobby. As she walked out of the bank's front door, her worst nightmare was walking through it.

"Sabrina," Jeff spoke, holding the door for her to pass. She pretended not to hear him and kept walking to her car. She hopped inside, put the car in reverse, and hoped she would never have to see him again.

31

Jeff had taken a few days off from work to clear his head and to figure out what in the hell was going on with his daughter. This morning's workout helped lighten some of the stress, but his mind was still in a whirlwind. Not realizing before last night that Deandra was still mourning the death of her mother, had his soul aching. There was nothing he could do to heal her pain, yet he didn't want to continue to ignore her cries for help. He concluded that her acting out was her way of getting attention. He decided it was time for some counseling, and figured it wouldn't hurt to even sit in on a few sessions with his daughter and gain some insight into how Denise's death was affecting her. He had planned to make the call right after leaving the bank. That was until he bumped into Sabrina. It had been on his mind to reach out. He felt he owed her an apology for simply dismissing her from their life when all she had ever done was be a friend. He was actually even starting to miss her random pop-ups. Maybe he could have confided in her about his daughter. A woman's perspective was always enlightening.

Now as he sat in his car, parked in front of her house, he worried his apology wouldn't be enough to win back her friendship, considering how she deliberately had ignored him at the bank. He had given her the cold shoulder one too many times and she was obviously reciprocating the favor. Done with the twisted mind games, he was going to be the better person. But he was also going to make it perfectly clear that he did not want any further involvement in her relationship. A peaceful platonic friendship was all he desired.

He stepped out of his car and went for what he knew. Her car wasn't in the driveway so he figured she had parked it in the garage, like usual. He ran his left palm over his fresh cut and approached the door, throwing caution to the wind. It never crossed his mind what he would say if her husband was home. He'd manufacture that lie when he crossed that bridge.

Is this really the right thing to do? he pondered before ringing the doorbell. He rang it again. When no one responded, he knocked on the door and waited. Either no one was home or she really didn't want to be bothered by him. Getting the message, he turned to leave. Before he could get halfway to his car, a man's voice called after him. He turned back around to find her husband waving for him to come back.

"Shit!" he hissed under his breath. *I didn't expect this motherfucker to be home*, he thought. He put on a fake smile and retraced his steps.

"How's it going?" Luke said, seemingly out of breath. He wiped his hands on a white cloth as Jeff approached the door.

Jeff cleared his throat and reached in to shake Luke's hand. "What's up, man?" he said nervously.

"Sorry I didn't hear the doorbell. I was on a conference call."

"No worries, man. I ugh…hope I didn't disturb anything."

"Not at all." Luke smiled.

"I was hoping your wife was home. It's my daughter," Jeff lied. "She's having some trouble at the new dance school…and uh…I can't seem to get her to talk to me about what's going on."

"Explain no more. I don't have any children, but I know all too well what it's like trying to figure out what's going on in a woman's head," Luke chortled.

Jeff laughed along. "Exactly!"

"Come on in. She just ran a quick errand."

"Are you sure?" Jeff looked back at his car. "I can come back later."

Luke opened the door wider and allowed him inside. "It's perfectly all right. I could use some company."

Jeff walked inside of a house he was all too familiar with, yet he pretended it was his first time in the Montgomerys' home.

"This is a lot of space you have here," Jeff said, looking around as Luke trailed behind.

"Yeah…that was Sabrina's doing. I'm a little more on the conservative side, if you will."

Jeff nodded his head in agreement. "I'm the same way, man. All about simplicity." Jeff walked down the long hall and into the living room. His eyes began to roam in puzzlement. The living room looked much different than he recalled. There were boxes piled high in every corner, and white sheets covered most of the furniture.

"Excuse the mess," Luke said.

"Looks like you guys are moving."

Luke cleared a path for Jeff to walk in. "Actually, we're painting and remodeling."

"Gotcha!" Jeff headed over to one of the covered sofas and took a seat.

"If you'll excuse me for a minute, I'll text Sabrina and let her know you're here."

"Thanks, man!' Jeff hollered back as Luke's footsteps trailed off. He couldn't believe he was actually sitting here like a fool on this man's couch, waiting on his wife to come home. Jeff shook his head. This was more than a bold-ass move, and knowing Sabrina, she was going to freak the hell out once she walked through that door. He chided himself for accepting the invitation. More nervous than a lab rat, he mentally debated whether he should stick around.

He rubbed his sweaty palms over his jeans as he heard Luke walking back into the living room. He stood up. "You know what, I just remembered I have to be somewhere in an hour," he lied.

Luke grinned sinisterly before revealing the small, black caliber handgun. He pointed it right at Jeff's torso.

"Man, what the fuck!" Jeff exclaimed as his hands automatically flew up in the air.

"Sit!" Luke ordered.

Jeff bit his bottom lip in rage as he did as he was told. He lowered his hands and balled his fists tightly at his sides. Every angry breath he took felt like spitballs of fire shooting out of his nose and ears. His breathing intensified and his only clear thought was, *If he shoots, he'd better kill me.*

"You're one cocky son-of-a-bitch waltzing up in here as if I'm completely oblivious to the fact that you're fucking my *wife!*"

Jeff's face was muddled with anger. His breathing deepened and his blood boiled furiously.

"I don't know what you're talking about, but what I do know is that you better—"

"I better what?" Luke challenged. He walked closer to Jeff and planted the gun in the middle of his forehead. "Last I checked, I'm the one holding the gun."

"What do you want from me, man?"

Luke laughed heartily. It wasn't until then that Jeff noticed the white powdery residue clinging to Luke's nose.

"I want revenge, you dirty motherfucker!"

Jeff only stared at him, his upper lip curled in annoyance.

"I don't want your wife!" he said, reassuring Luke.

"Now you insult me?" Luke clapped the gun hard against Jeff's head causing blood to instantly squirt onto the white sheets draping the furniture.

"Awwwww!" Jeff howled in pain, holding the left side of his head.

"You know, it amazes me how God can bless a scum asshole like you, and take from a noble man like me!"

Jeff winced in pain as blood poured down the left side of his face and onto his neck and shirt.

"I had dreams too!" Luke yelled, his voice booming with every word. "I was rebuilding my life after losing my son, until your wife...*your wife*," he said painfully, jamming the gun back into the center of Jeff's forehead, "came along and destroyed *everything*." He took a couple of steps back and snatched down his pants and underwear. "You see what that rotting, no-driving bitch of yours did to me?"

Jeff looked on in confusion and disbelief as Luke exposed what was left of his penis.

"Don't sit there and act like you don't remember the car accident that killed your wife and left several critically injured."

Jeff narrowed his disbelieving eyes. In hindsight, he could never forget that fateful day he lost Denise, but the excruciating pain in his head and the burn in his chest overrode his nostalgia, and instead, fueled his anger to attack the no-dick bastard.

"Well, I'm one of the injured, you slimy son-of-a-bitch!"

Jeff took a deep breath. "Please, man," he implored. "I'm sorry that happened to you, but I had nothing to do with that."

"The same way you're sorry about fucking my wife? Or didn't you have anything to do with that either?" Jeff's silence returned. "I didn't think so." Luke paused. "The only way to make this right, is to take everything from you that she took from me," he admonished.

Jeff closed his eyes. He was no chump and he refused to go down without a fight. As Luke leveled the gun and cocked it, Jeff jumped off the sofa and lunged for it. The gun went off and Jeff knew right away that he had been shot.

32

Sabrina was turning her key in the door when she heard a loud shot ring out. She knew there was trouble once she spotted Jeff's car in the front of her house, yet she still hoped Luke hadn't done anything foolish. As she ran into the living room, she saw Jeff lying on the floor and her husband hovering over him. She didn't know if Jeff was hurt or not. She began to panic, fearing the worse.

"Luke, what the hell are you doing?" Sabrina walked slowly around her husband, her eyes fretfully jumping from him to Jeff.

"Look who decided to join the party," Luke bantered wickedly. She stared at her husband wide-eyed, thinking he'd gone insane. Her heart didn't stop racing until Jeff's eyes met hers and she saw that he wasn't severely hurt.

"Your boyfriend here decided he wanted to drop by and spend a little time with us." Luke swiped at the blood dripping from his nose.

"Luke, please," Sabrina begged. "Don't do this. It's not worth it."

Luke eyed her incredulously. "You think I'm supposed to let this arrogant prick walk out of here, alive?"

"Let's stick to the plan, baby. Please," Sabrina pleaded, tears welling in her eyes.

"Speaking of which…go ahead and tell him the good news, honey," Luke urged.

"Luke, you're high," Sabrina said. He uttered something in Spanish that she couldn't comprehend. "Please don't do this." She shook her head, pleading with her husband as best she could.

"Don't do what exactly? Tell Mr. Cockiness here how *we* strung him along long enough to impregnate you." He peered down at Jeff. "I bet all this time you thought it was your cock doing all the work," he tittered. "Sorry to disappoint you, sunny boy!"

Jeff shot Sabrina a malicious and disgusted look. She diverted her eyes, barely able to look at him.

"Or don't tell him how I personally selected this house so that we could slowly rob him of his future the way his wife did mine." Luke sneered, grabbing her and Jeff's attention all at once.

At first Sabrina didn't realize what Luke meant, but then, all the missing pieces started coming together for her. She stared at Luke with disappointment all over her face. She had not known that it had been Jeff's wife who had caused the accident that nearly killed Luke that day. Sabrina's right hand covered her mouth. This was all a setup from day one. This was never *only* about them having another baby. This was solely about him getting revenge.

"So you played me, too, huh?" Sabrina said.

"Awww, sweetie. Don't look at it that way. I knew if I told you, you would never go along with it. I did it for us," he lamented. He looked down at her belly. "It was always for us, Sabrina."

Suddenly they heard the front door open and a woman's voice called out for Sabrina.

"Mrs. Montgomery, I'm here to tour the property!" she announced.

When their unexpected visitor rounded the corner, Luke got distracted and turned the gun on her.

"Oh my God! Please don't shoot!" the woman yelled frantically. Her eyes darted from Jeff to Sabrina and then back to a gun-holding

Luke. "Please. Please. Don't shoot. I was inquiring about the ad online…I don't want to get involved in this." She closed her eyes tightly. "I didn't see anything! Please don't kill me!" she cried. She began praying aloud.

"Shut the hell up!" Luke screamed, waving the gun in her direction.

Welcoming the distraction, Jeff pulled Luke down to the floor by his legs and wrestled the gun out of his hand. Two shots rang out and the woman screamed for mercy as she raced back down the hall and out of the door she had entered. Sabrina blazed that trail with her, escaping the scene before police were called out. She watched the woman hop in her car and speed off, and she did the same. She wasn't going to jail.

"Nine-one-one. What is your emergency?" the operator spoke.

Sabrina's cell nearly fell out of her trembling hands. "Please send police before someone gets killed!" she said hysterically.

"Ma'am, I need you to calm down and tell me what's going on."

"He's going to kill him!" she screamed.

"Who's going to kill who? Can you provide me with a description of the suspect and an address so that I can send over a unit?"

Sabrina rattled off Ms. Rester's address. "He's tall…black," she said, tears pouring down her cheeks. Her stomach began to churn and she ended the call before the operator could ask her for anything more. She pulled over on the side of the service road, opened her door and vomited. Cars flew past her, a few honking in passing.

"Agcccckk, accckkk!" She coughed. She slowly came to and shut the door, her head spinning from all the madness that had transpired. As much as she wanted to go back to rescue Luke, she couldn't. What if the cops were already there? What if they were waiting for her return so that they could lure them both off to jail? She couldn't risk it, for the sake of her "unborn child." Luke would understand that. She hoped.

She got on the highway headed in the west direction. Fear and paranoia had her constantly looking in her rearview mirror, expecting the police to be trailing her. She didn't know where she was going, but she wasn't turning back. Luke had brought this all on himself and as much as she loved her husband, this was one mess he had to find his own way out of.

Tears filled her eyes as she thought about what would happen to him. She hit the steering wheel repeatedly and screamed at the top of her lungs. She drove for miles in deep thought. She didn't stop crying until she was parked outside of her parents' massive mansion. It was the last place she wanted to be, but they were the only ones who would protect her.

33

"Don't you ever threaten me, motherfucker!" Jeff had yelled just before his right fist collided with Luke's jaw. "You ain't so tough now, you little bitch!" He hit him with a quick and precise uppercut, causing one of Luke's teeth to fly right out of his mouth. Jeff didn't stop hitting him until Luke's newly discolored eyes were bulging out of their sockets. Only then did he catch a breather as sweat and blood began to burn his own eyes. Blood had splattered everywhere, including on Jeff's shirt and shoes. He double-blinked to try to clear the mess that was blurring his vision out of his eyes. When that didn't work, he lifted the tail of his shirt and tried to remove the blood with it.

Once Jeff's vision grew clearer, he looked back down at a motionless Luke. His swelling eyes were bloodied with black and purple rings around them and his usual small nose was slightly crooked. There was no doubt that it looked like he had been double-teamed in a bare-fisted boxing match with Mike Tyson and Floyd Mayweather. It was a horrific, gory sight. By the time the cops barged through the front door, Luke was lying on the floor, clearly unconscious.

It was a like a scene in the movie the way the events unfolded, and Jeff found himself caught red-handed with a gun in his hand, aimed at a defenseless white man who had been practically beaten to death. It didn't look good and his only two witnesses had torn their asses, leaving him in a damnable situation with his life and freedom on the line.

The first officer on the scene rushed over to Jeff and ordered him to place his hands behind his back.

"I didn't do anything!" Jeff shouted to the cop.

"Hands behind your back!" the officer yelled again.

"I'm not going to jail! This man tried to kill me! I was defending myself!"

The second officer trained his weapon on Jeff the entire time. He looked down at Luke and then at Jeff. He eyed Jeff in contempt as he instantly called for backup.

"I said, hands behind your back! Don't make me use force!" the officer yelled again.

"This shit ain't right!" Jeff protested as he resisted arrest. "That man tried to kill me! There were two women here who saw the entire thing. I'm not going to jail for something I did not do. I want a lawyer!"

"I'm going to ask you one last time to place your hands behind your fucking back!"

Once Jeff realized that the two white officers didn't believe one second of his story, he reluctantly obliged. Recalling the story he had seen on the news last week where an innocent black man was wrongly killed by Dallas police, he dropped his head, not wanting the same fate. The big-nosed cop roughly placed the handcuffs on Jeff while reading him his Miranda rights. Nervous energy swirled through Jeff's system. Why was this happening to him? He should have known Sabrina was nothing but trouble, yet here again, he realized he had ignored all the telltale signs.

A few short minutes later, another set of officers joined the scene along with the paramedics. Jeff watched in repulsion, fearing the worst, but hoping he had not just killed the man who medics were carefully loading onto the gurney. Luke's face was unrecognizable while only Jeff's swollen fists and head equally pained from the blows he had delivered and received. He needed medical attention as well, but not as urgently as Luke.

Jeff was mortified as he was shamefully escorted out of the Montgomerys' house in handcuffs, while Luke on the other hand was wheeled out on a gurney and placed in an ambulance to be transported to the hospital.

"Watch your head," the officer said as he put Jeff in the backseat of his squad car. He closed the door and went to converse with the other officers who had joined the scene. Out of all the years Jeff lived in this neighborhood, this had been his first encounter with the police. He hadn't so much as gotten a ticket; that's how much he was a law-abiding citizen. So to be in this predicament had him totally disconcerted.

"Fuck!" Jeff allowed his aching head to fall back against the seat. His mind was spinning in a million directions as he slowly began to realize how much trouble he might be in. He would need a paid lawyer, and a damn good one at that. When he finally raised his head and gazed out of the right window, he met eyes with several of the neighbors who had come out of the sweet confines of their homes to witness the atrocity taking place.

"Mr. Jackson!" a young boy yelled through the window as he rolled up on the squad car on his bicycle. "What happened to you?" he inquired, peeking through the glass.

Jeff looked up and had recognized the boy instantly. It was one of Deandra's classmates. "*Shit!*" he hissed. Jeff had no earthly idea what time it was but if Erik was already riding his bike, that meant Deandra was likely already off the school bus. He tried to wiggle his way out of the restraints but it was impossible. They were so tight it nearly cut off his circulation. His cell phone began to ring.

As he suspected, it was Deandra's ringtone. He panted as he struggled, kicking the backseat in frustration. A short moment later, the two officers got back in the car.

"All right, buddy. Time to go downtown."

34

"Thanks for all your help, Pamela. And yes, I will definitely let you know when my fiancé and I begin the house search." Nadine pulled the phone slightly away from her ear once Belinda walked into her office. "Give me one second," she whispered to her receptionist.

"Congratulations, again," Pamela said. "I'll be on the lookout for my wedding invite."

Nadine simply went along with the flow. Little did Pamela know, there wouldn't be a wedding because she and Leonard had agreed to elope. Nadine stifled a laugh. "You betcha! Talk to you soon," she said before disconnecting the call. She peered up at Belinda who was flawless in a hip-hugging black skirt and matching blazer that accentuated her strong curves. She had an admirable fashion sense and her hair and makeup was always so glamorous, which is why Nadine looked forward to getting her opinion on the wedding dress she had ordered online. Although she and Leonard weren't technically having a wedding, Nadine still wanted a beautiful white dress, similar to the one she had always dreamed of wearing on her special day. She had found it days ago after a long day and night of Internet surfing. She had it rushed to her Aunt Mickey's house in Atlanta and she had already started working on the alterations.

"Awww…what's the sad face for?"

Belinda walked closer to Nadine's desk and took a seat directly across from her. "I have a major dilemma," she stressed, "and I could really use your advice." She pulled her long Brazilian curls away from her face, exposing more of her beautiful brown skin.

"Sure! I'm all ears." Nadine scooted her chair up more and placed her hands on her desk. She interlocked her fingers, giving Belinda her undivided attention.

Belinda took a deep breath and her eyes fluttered as she prepared to present her situation. "I have a friend who's getting ready to make the biggest mistake of her life," she said flatly.

Nadine widened her eyes and tilted her head slightly. "How so?"

"Well…she's getting married."

Nadine's perfectly arched eyebrows crinkled in puzzlement.

"That's not all," Belinda continued. "She's getting married to an extremely deceitful man."

Nadine inhaled a deep breath. "Wow! What exactly is he being dishonest about?" she curiously inquired.

Belinda shifted apprehensively in her seat as if this was a difficult conversation.

"His health." Belinda's eyes broke away shortly before finding their way back. "He's misleading her by not telling her that he's HIV positive."

Nadine's right hand flew to her chest in shock. "Whoa!" That nearly knocked the breath out of her lungs. She measured the look in Belinda's eyes and could sense her serious concern for her friend. The only problem was, Nadine wasn't sure on how to respond. "That's very serious," Nadine retorted. She shook her head as she put herself in Belinda's shoes.

"I love her like a sister and I don't want to see her get hurt by this man. I don't. But it would devastate her if she had to find out from me."

"Assuming she doesn't know what she's getting herself into, I feel as a friend you're privileged in that role to bring this to her attention so that she doesn't marry this joker under false pretenses."

Belinda nodded her understanding.

"Whewww…HIV of all things," Nadine continued, processing what Belinda had shared with her. "How did you receive this information? And are you certain that it is in fact HIV?"

Belinda's face seemingly tightened as her eyes spread. "In all honesty, I worked in the doctor's office that her fiancé went to. I had access to his medical records and I know for a fact he was one of our infected patients."

Nadine's face nearly melted. "What kind of man keeps something like *that* from his wife?" she asked in disgust. "That's a pretty heavy burden," she added.

"A man who's afraid of being alone," Belinda replied. "A man who looks, acts, and feels so…perfect."

Nadine sighed.

"I realize it's a sensitive situation, which is why I can't seem to bring myself to tell her. What if she doesn't believe me? What if I go to jail for sharing confidential medical records. What if…"

Nadine handed her a tissue as tears began to flood from her eyes.

"What if I sabotage the best thing that could ever happen to her? What if she's more accepting of that than I am and decides to cut *me* off for intruding on her relationship?" Belinda blotted both her eyes with the tissue.

"It's okay," Nadine said consolingly as more and more tears reeled from Belinda's bright, amber-colored eyes, ruining her makeup.

"I'm in such a pickle. I really don't know what to do," Belinda admitted. "I was hoping you could tell me."

Nadine stiffened in her seat. Her eyes lost themselves as she waited for the answer to come to her. "It's a tough one, Belinda." She cleared her throat. "Part of me feels that as a friend, you're obligated to tell her, while the other half of me feels it's not your place to invade his privacy and meddle in their personal affairs."

"So basically, I'm damned if I do and damned if I don't," Belinda brazenly conceded.

"Look at it this way. If she's really a friend, she would never hold that against you. Don't beat yourself up about not wanting to jeopardize your freedom for your friendship. There's more at stake."

Belinda smiled. "Thanks, boss!"

"You're always welcome, dear."

Belinda seemed relieved. She stood up from the chair and sighed. "While I'm still torn, I do feel like a major weight has been lifted off my shoulders."

Nadine smiled softly. "Pray about it."

Belinda tilted her head to one side and smiled. "You know what. That's exactly what I'm going to do." With that, she turned to leave.

Nadine sat in deep thought long enough to realize it was way past her time to go. She picked up the phone and dialed Jim's extension.

"Jim speaking."

"Hey, I'm going to wrap things up and head out. Did you need me to stop by the office before I leave?"

"Nope. I think I've got everything covered for the hearing to-morrow."

"Okay. Please extend my deepest sympathies to Mr. McCormick's wife again. She's obviously still dealing with the loss of her husband and now to have to fight his ex-wife, mistress, and children in court over his estate can be extremely taxing on one's health." She sighed. "Poor woman."

"Tell me about it. My vindictive and ungrateful ex-wife did a similar thing to me and she damn sure didn't wait until I was pushing up dandelions to do it. That's why I've sworn to never remarry," he declared.

"Awww come on, Jim. Don't give up on love."

"Tsk. The verdict is still out on if love really exists. I'm no more of a believer of love than I am of extraterrestrials."

Nadine couldn't help but chuckle at his last comment. She shouldn't be listening to any of this. She was getting married in a few short weeks and all this negative nonsense that she was circuitously receiving was only going to cause her to question if she was truly ready to jump the broom. She loved Leonard. He was the one for her and why she wasn't going to dare speak ill thoughts into the universe. It would only jinx their relationship.

"All right, Mr. Cynical Romantic. Call me after court and let me know how it went."

"You bet your bottom dollar I will."

Nadine couldn't disconnect the call fast enough. She looked out the window and saw that the rain had completely stopped. If she was going to jet, now was the perfect time. As she cleared her desk and prepared for takeoff, her cell began to ring. She sighed. "What now." She swept up the phone and looked peculiarly at the screen. She didn't recognize the number. Hoping it wasn't a client calling this late, she pressed the *TALK* button anyway. "This is Nadine."

"Nadine, it's me. I need your help."

She stopped everything she was doing and stood rigidly in place. "Jeff?"

"I wasn't given long to talk. I'm in a little bit of a bind and I need you to get me out of here."

"Get you out of what? Where are you?" She was caught completely off guard by the call.

"I'm in jail."

"Be careful to whom you entrust your heart. Most of the world is in search of not love, but an impossible concept: eternal infatuation."

—Author Unknown

35

"Jail!" Nadine blurted.

That was one word no man wanted to hear, and definitely not an innocent man. Jeff sighed deeply. Nadine was the last person he wanted to call and invite into his madness, but he found himself dialing her number anyway. He could visualize the look on her face and damn near read her mind that very second. She sounded as shocked as he was. *Damn*, he thought. He dropped his head in disgrace and tried to tune out all the noise building around him.

"What the hell are you doing in jail?" she continued to quiz.

"Look, I will explain everything later. I need you to come bail me out. Don't worry about the money. I'll pay you back."

"Pssst. You are so unbelievable."

"Nadine, please!" He didn't have time for this shit. The last thing he needed was a lecture and her dredging up the past.

The other side of the line grew silent as Jeff rattled off specific details on whom she needed to contact to find out what his bail had been set at.

"Time!" the guard called out.

Jeff looked behind him and bounced his head in acknowledgment. He held up one finger, begging with his eyes for another minute.

"Wait, shouldn't your fiancée be handling this business for you?" Nadine boldly countered.

Jeff's skin tightened and his breathing became harder to manage as her rancorous rage strangled him through the phone line. "Can you do it or not?" he implored mercifully.

"I'll see what I can do," Nadine retorted. "But don't hold your breath," she said before ending his call.

Jeff slowly placed the phone back on its hook. The guard standing merely inches away from him slapped the cuffs back on without further delay. He escorted him back to the holding cell. Jeff swept his eyes over the jailhouse. He refused to stay there overnight, but if Nadine didn't push her ill feelings to the side, he would have no other choice.

The cuffs came off and Jeff rejoined his cellmates who were all tending to their own. Though he had never stepped one foot inside a jail, he watched enough court TV and had heard enough stories to know to keep his guard up and to mind his own business. Bearing that in mind, he barely made eye contact as he passed a tall, burly, white man wearing a wife beater and jeans. He was engaged in some heavy conversation with another brother who dressed like he had just left the motherland. Jeff overheard the white guy admit to stabbing his own brother ninety-six times after a heated argument, and the other claimed he was racially profiled and brought in for past traffic violations.

"I was just sitting at a red light, minding my own business when they came out of nowhere flashing me down. It's a conspiracy against the black man," the brotha hollered.

Jeff took a seat on the hard bench and allowed his pounding head to make a pillow out of the cement-brick wall. He closed his eyes and tried to imagine being anywhere else but here.

"Might as well make yourself comfortable," he heard someone say. He popped his eyes back open and the young brotha who had been standing in the far-right corner with a black hoodie concealing most of his face, was now seated next to him.

"'Sup," Jeff said, not really up for small talk.

"Ain't nothing. What they bring you down for? Tickets?" he asked.

Jeff shook his head. He wished that was the case. "In all honesty, man, I really don't know why the hell I'm in here."

The young brother *tsked*. "I understand. You're innocent just like the rest of us motherfuckers." He laughed. "Well, let them tell it, I burglarized someone's house. Them fools say they got me on caaaamera and shiiiit. Hell, I'm innocent until proven guilty, ya know what I'm sayin'. They ain't caught me on camera doin' nothin'." He laughed again.

Jeff eyed him strangely, not comprehending why the young man who looked to be no more than twenty, found such serious charges funny. "Hope everything works out for you, man." He really didn't know what else to say.

"True dat. True dat," the youngster replied, bouncing his head with every other word.

Jeff looked up at the clock above them. This was going to be a long night.

36

After posting Jeff's $5,000 bail a few hours ago, Nadine waited anxiously for his phone call. Hearing his voice right now would at least put her mind somewhat at ease in knowing that he was all right. While he could be the biggest ass sometimes, jail was no place for Jeff, and as hard as she tried, she couldn't wrap her mind around how he managed to end up there.

As if sensing her worry, Canvas climbed on the couch next to her.

"Mama," he said, placing his small sticky hands on Nadine's cheeks.

"Hey, my little man," she sang, kissing him on both cheeks. She stared at him for a moment. He looked so much like his father. If Jeff never got anything else right in his life, this he did. As she played with her son, it hit her to check on Deandra. God forbid that child was home alone. She hurriedly dialed Deandra's cell. When she didn't answer, panic set in. She called her grandmother, Grace.

"Chello," Grace answered.

"Hello, Ms. Grace. This is Nadine."

Silence.

"Grace?"

"I can hear mighty fine. What's the purpose of this call," Grace spat nastily, clearly hanging on to the past.

Nadine almost hung up the phone and let it be. This was not her battle anymore.

"I'm calling to check on Deandra. Is she there with you?"

"No, she's not."

"Okay, sorry to bother you," Nadine said. "I'll call her cell again."

"She won't answer it because that daddy of hers took it from her."

"I see." Nadine immediately stood from the couch and began gathering her purse and Canvas's bag. "Well, I won't keep you—"

"Wait! Now you ain't neva call me fo' anything, but you call me for *this*. Are you still sniffing up Jeff's ass?"

"Excuse me?" Nadine was taken aback by the disrespect.

"Chile, don't try to act all brand-new with me. Ya might think I'm old and senile, but I'm shonuff hip to your homewrecking ass!"

Nadine was fuming now.

"You had him all to yourself when my daughter was alive; must you chase behind him while she's dead too? It was trash like you that drove me and my Vernon apart. Can't find a man of your own so you steal another's!"

"I am not about to listen to this nonsense tonight. I called because I was concerned about Deandra's welfare. All this…" She took another deep breath. "I won't stand for it. You will not disrespect me and blame me for your daughter's faults! We resolved our issues and that's all you need to know!" With that she dismissed the call. Had she knew the attack was coming, she would not have crossed over into enemy territory. "The nerve of that woman!" Her heart raced as she walked around the loft searching for her keys. "And she calls herself a Christian!" Nadine saw nothing but red. That's how upset Grace made her. "Where'd you hide Mommy's keys?" she asked Canvas. "Keys. Where's Mommy's keys?" Canvas looked at her smiling. She searched high and low until she stopped and realized that they were in her hands.

She scooped up her son and headed out the door. If Deandra wasn't with Grace, there was a strong possibility that she was at home all alone.

37

"You can let me out right here, my man," Jeff told the cab driver. As the car came to a complete stop directly in front of Sabrina's house, Jeff dug in his pockets and fished out two twenties and a ten-dollar bill. "Here you go. Keep the change."

"Thank you, sir," the driver replied as Jeff climbed out of the passenger seat he had been adamant about sitting in. After the events that took place earlier, he realized he was a tad bit of a claustrophobe. He didn't care for riding in backseats and he sure as hell didn't like being in tight confined spaces like jail cells. It nearly drove him insane. To experience the outside world again, fresh air and freedom had him profoundly grateful. It was the simple things in life he had foolishly taken for granted.

The driver slowly pulled away from the curb, leaving Jeff alone in the wee hours of the morning. Jeff pulled out his keys to his car and disarmed the alarm. He needed to get to his baby girl whom he was worried sick about.

Ignoring the twenty miles-per-hour speed limit, he whipped around the corner and drove a couple miles up the road. The first thing he spotted when he turned on his street had him stretching his neck out like a chicken. He narrowed his eyes and zoomed in on Nadine's car, which was unexpectedly parked in his driveway. He killed the engine and hopped out of the car, a cool breeze flirting along his sticky skin.

Jeff couldn't make it to his door fast enough. When he walked inside the quiet house, a pungent odor attacked his nose. The farther he walked inside, he realized it was only burnt popcorn. He walked right past the kitchen and headed straight to Deandra's room. He needed to lay eyes on his daughter. Needed to make sure she was perfectly okay.

Jeff stuck his head in the door and found Deandra and Canvas asleep in the bed and Nadine situated on the huge bean bag chair with a pink-and-white Barbie blanket pulled up to her neck. His heart began to beat normal again as he laid eyes on his children and Nadine. They were peacefully asleep and he had Nadine to thank for that.

Not wanting to disturb their rest, Jeff quietly closed the door and retreated to his bedroom. A long, hot shower was way overdue. He had only been in jail a few hours, but he smelled like he had been inside for an eternity.

After indulging in the longest shower he had ever taken in his life, he decided to watch some television, in hopes that it would take his mind off of everything that went down earlier; if only temporarily. It had crossed his mind several times that he might have killed a man. The thought of facing a murder rap was hard to swallow. As a plethora of scenarios played in his mind, Jeff's body began to tense. He would need a damn good lawyer and an even better defense that could justify his position. He rechanneled his attention toward the light footsteps as they pattered down the long corridor. He looked up and Nadine's alluring silhouette appeared in his doorway.

"May I come in?" she asked gingerly.

"You're always welcome in here," he replied with a sheepish grin, meaning every word of it.

"Whatever," she retorted sarcastically, closing the door behind her.

Jeff's eyes fought the temptation lurking around him as he watched her ample ass switch past him in a melodic dubstep. Her superpowers having pussy was calling his name while the sweet smell of her perfume provoked all his senses. She might have been off limits for now, but the ambitious swing of her ass fighting for a victory against those skinny jeans continued to materialize every dirty thought in his head. It was no surprise; Nadine had always had this effect on him and she must have known it to claim the spot on the chaise lounge clear across the room.

"I don't bite," he said flirtatiously. She completely ignored his comment.

"Sooooooo…" she began, sliding a shirt strap back over her shoulder. With her back slightly against the chair, she shifted her legs to one side and crossed her feet.

Jeff muted the television and met her attention. He knew exactly what this conversation was going to be about so there was no reason to feign ignorance. His only issue was that she wanted to have the talk at two o'clock in the morning.

"First off, let me say thank you," he began. He would have liked to thank her in other ways, but given the tragic interruption of their former status quo, the good old-fashioned way would keep him out of enemy territory. Another round of drama over a woman was the last thing he needed in his life. "You didn't have to post my bail and you definitely didn't have to come over here and stay with Deandra, but you did…and from the bottom of my heart, it's greatly appreciated," he said in all seriousness. "I owe you one."

Her right eyebrow raised a bit, but her soft angelic lips of gold curled into an assuring smile. "You're welcome," she fathomed. She held that incomplete look on her face.

It was evident Nadine wanted more ass kissing. More explanation. More clarification on what had happened that resulted in her rushing to be *here* and not *there*. Never-ending questions danced in her eyes and Jeff held every last one of the keys. Instead of giving in to exactly what she wanted, which was for him to put all his business on front street, he took in the breathtaking view and allowed her to wallow in her assumptions. She would never believe him if he told her the truth of how he was set up by a scandalous woman and her no-dick-having husband who plotted to steal his sperm and wreck his life because of Denise. Hell, he wouldn't even believe that story. And as he thought about it now, he hoped Sabrina wasn't pregnant. He couldn't recall one time where the rubber had broken. Luke had to be fucking with his head. Had to be.

"I hope I didn't get you into any trouble with your old man," Jeff lied. It was a lame attempt to soften the awkwardness floating between them.

Nadine tightened her lips and inhaled sharply. The look on her face sent a chill rushing down his spine. She was reading right through him.

"I appreciate your concern but rest assured, it was no trouble at all. Quite the opposite actually." She relinquished a contradicting smirk. This was verbal foul play but Jeff had already submerged himself inside her love pool and was in too deep to pull out. Besides, the more her lips moved, the harder his pine got. Drowning like a fool when he knew how to swim was worth it. "You see, Leonard is quite an understanding guy, which in fact is the *only* reason I ran to your rescue." Her impish smile hung like a poster on her face. "So you can thank *him* later."

She played dirtier than he thought. Jeff shot her a smug look before completely diverting his eyes.

"Since that's out of the way, now can we address the huge pink elephant in the room?" she asked.

As nasty as she was being toward him, he still wanted to take that trip down memory lane. It would ease his mind and satisfy him greatly if he could climb inside of her paradise and reclaim what was his. Remind her of what she'd been missing, and at the same time, punish that pussy for straying away from home. Jeff turned back to her.

"I got into a physical altercation with some guy," he relented.

Her sultry brown eyes never wavered as she patiently waited for the rest of the story. He shrugged his shoulders. "That's it." That was about as much information he felt like sharing right now.

Nadine released a frustrating sigh.

"I'll have your money first thing in the morning once the bank opens," he added. "I can—"

"So you're not going to tell me everything?" she asked, cutting him off.

"It's nothing to worry about. It's my problem; I'll deal with it." She dropped her head and began to massage her temple. That's when he noticed it. His forehead crinkled in confusion and disappointment. "Doesn't look like I'm the only one holding out."

She raised her head. "What are you talking about?"

"The ring."

Nadine looked down at her left hand in surprise, her mouth slightly agape. "I...uh...was going to tell you...I didn't..." she said, stumbling over her words.

"Bullshit! Because if you wanted me to know I would have known way before now."

"Really?" She held both hands in the air. "I can't keep doing this with you," she said flippantly.

"Doing what?" Jeff swore he had fire coming out of his eyes.

"I can't keep allowing you to make me feel guilty about my happiness!"

"I've already told you. You're moving way too fast with this guy! You barely even know him!"

"Like I knew you?" she shot sarcastically. "Pssst…gimme a break! And why you're so quick to criticize me for who *I* choose to marry, I suggest you put that same amount of energy into your own damn relationships. Hell, I don't recall you asking me for *my* approval on your fiancée, but you want to police mine! And since we're on the subject, why isn't *she* here?"

He could see it in her eyes. She still loved him. She still cared. There was no way he was wrong about this. He pulled his bottom lip in and nodded his head. It was time he put an end to this war.

"Nadine, I am not engaged. And on that note, I don't plan to be anytime soon. What you heard, better yet what you *think* you know, is all a lie. A lie that could have been cleared up a long damn time ago, but you never gave me a chance to do so."

She shook her head and pursed her lips in a fashion that spoke volumes. However, when she crossed her arms and cocked her head to one side, it was plain as day that she didn't believe one word falling from his mouth. Still, he carried on.

"But of course it's too much of an inconvenience to believe me now because then you'd have to admit that you're marrying this chump to get back at me!"

Her eyes widened incredulously. "So is that what you really think?" she guffawed. She double-blinked and every angry line in her face slowly softened as he ripped off the mask she'd been wearing. "Don't flatter yourself, Jeff Jackson."

They had much in common, and pride had been chief of their problems. But for what it was worth, he loved the hell out of Nadine and he knew she still loved him. It was written all over her face. He would bottle his concerns for now, but he definitely wasn't going to do it without getting one last thing off his chest.

"If you're happy, I'm happy," he said lastly. "Just know, when he fucks up, I'll be right here waiting."

38

Leonard had come home to an empty house tonight. As unsettling as it was, Nadine was not the type of woman to
leave a friend stranded in their time of need. So it was no
surprise when she asked if he would be okay with her posting Jeff's
bail. They didn't discuss the particulars, but he was sure she would
bring him up to speed once she got home.

He turned over and saw that it was almost four in the morning.
He couldn't sleep a wink without her and Canvas there; not to
mention, his best friend had dropped the bomb on him earlier today.
For some strange reason, Greg believed that Vivian had shot him.
Leonard had heard outlandish allegations before, but this one
took the cake. He could only wonder why Greg would say such
nonsense about his wife after all she had done for him. Was he
that angry with her for putting him in a nursing home? Was this
his way of getting even with her? The more Leonard replayed
their conversation in his mind, the more he tossed and turned. It
had to be the new medication they had him on, he thought. Had
to be. He refused to believe that his friend could be that damn
malicious.

"Come on, Greg. Keep a level head, man," Leonard had said. "It's
these pills got you talking like this."

"It's...not...the...damn pills!" Greg protested adamantly. "I told
you...that *bitch*...wants me...dead!" he struggled.

Leonard could normally look a man in the eye and tell if he was lying, but when he looked at Greg, all he saw was a man with a vengeance rage. A man who refused to believe that he put the gun to his own damn head and pulled the trigger. Perhaps it was stress combined with the marital upheaval he was experiencing that had him convinced death would be much easier. But nonetheless, it was Greg who was responsible for this, not Vivian, and there was no way Leonard was going to stand by and watch Greg destroy everything he had in the process.

"A psychiatric hospital?" Leonard had repeated aloud and relentlessly in his mind as he sat across from Vivian in her and Greg's beautiful home. He had gone to see her in person immediately after visiting with Greg. She needed to know that her husband's mental state was taking him down a darker path than the one he had just gotten off of.

"It's for the best," she had said, crying on his shoulder. She was as surprised as Leonard that Greg would even accuse her of doing such a thing. "I may be a lot of things, but a murderer is not one of them!" She sniffled. "Just when I thought his memory was coming back," she added, "he takes a turn for the worse. The doctors warned me about this." She wept softly. "I didn't want to believe it would happen to my husband."

"Don't worry. We'll get him evaluated and if," he paused, managing his words carefully, "if it's determined he needs to be admitted, we'll proceed with that process," Leonard said, a tear crawling down his cheek. After seeing Greg in the condition he was in today, she now had his full support. He held her in his arms and consoled her the best way he knew how. This was hard on the both of them and while Greg and Vivian may not have seen eye to eye, Leonard knew deep down in his heart that she was not capable of hurting a fly.

After leaving Vivian alone in her thoughts, he asked one of the housekeepers to keep a special eye out on her. He had passed her his number and told her to call him if needed. With Vivian's tragic love affair with alcohol and prescription pills, he wouldn't doubt if she turned to either to self-medicate, and in a way, he almost wouldn't blame her.

Unable to sleep, Leonard slipped out of the bed and headed straight for the weight room. He needed to burn some steam and hitting a few sets would usually do the job. He had a lot on his mind, and with he and Nadine getting married soon, he needed to make sure he got a few things in check.

Thirty minutes into his workout, his doorbell rang. Leonard eased the bar off his shoulders and loaded it back onto the machine.

"Arghhh!" he bellowed as the burn in his arms and legs felt so good. He rushed down the stairs, knowing it was his beautiful Nadine. Sticky and sweaty, he wiped his forehead with the back of his hand before opening the door.

"Man, I…need…a place…to crash for…the night," Greg slurred.

Leonard's unbelieving eyes zeroed in on a disheveled Greg. "Man, are you kidding me?" Leonard poked his head out the door and began looking around. "Did you really escape from the damn nursing home?" His mouth fell agape as he studied his friend.

"Oooone…night," Greg said.

Leonard sighed deeply. "Shit, man!" He slowly opened the door and allowed Greg inside. He thought about calling Vivian but felt she would likely be in a drunken stupor by now. He'd wait until later that morning. "You can crash on the couch, man," Leonard said, eyeing Greg oddly.

"Stop…looking…at me…like…I'm fucking…nuts!"

"That's because you are!" Leonard shook his head disconcertedly. "Get some sleep," he said before treading back upstairs to his room. The stress had definitely returned stronger than ever.

39

With Canvas asleep in her left arm, Nadine struggled to keep from waking him as she inserted her key into the door. She had left Jeff's at the crack of dawn, hoping to make good timing to get Canvas off to daycare so that she could head to work. She was flying off of minimal sleep, and it didn't make it any better that she had an extremely important teleconference at nine and a meeting with a client at ten. She had a long day ahead of her, but it became interesting sooner than she imagined when she crept up the stairs and flipped on her room light.

"Agghhhh!" she screamed at the top of her lungs, frightening her son to the point of tears. The man coddling her favorite pillow and contaminating her bedsheets, hopped out of the bed. He threw up his hands. "Greg?" she said, confused as ever.

"I'm…sorry," Greg began. He stopped all at once and narrowed his eyes on Nadine.

"What's going on?" Leonard said, rushing into the room in a panic, practically out of breath. He twisted his face. "What part of catch the couch did you not hear?" he lashed out at Greg.

"It's okay," Nadine said. "Canvas and I can just get ready downstairs."

"That's not necessary. You can have my room," Leonard told her.

"It's you…" Greg began again. He tilted his head to the side. "Umbrella." He chuckled to himself.

Nadine looked away in embarrassment. There was an awkward energy rising between them.

Greg nodded his head. He looked at Leonard and then he looked at Nadine. "So this...is *her?*"

Leonard took a deep breath. "Greg, it's too early in the morning for this. I have court in another three hours and a client meeting. We can all catch up later," he said. He must have sensed her uneasiness.

Greg sat back down on the bed and began rubbing his head. "It's...all...coming back...now."

"What's coming back?" Leonard asked.

Greg met both of their eyes. "I...remember...*everything.*"

40

After speaking with Jacquelyn the night before about her plans to get the boys back, Naomi felt like she really had a support system after all. In the short time she'd been back in Texas, Charles' wife had become her sounding board, her sister, and even her confidante. She felt like she could talk to the woman about anything, and it helped greatly that Jacquelyn understood her. All they wanted was what was best for the children, and that was to see them back with their mother.

Naomi sprinkled baby powder in her silk panties and lathered on some unscented cocoa butter before spritzing on her and Greg's favorite perfume. She pulled her new dress over her head and modeled it in the mirror, her fabulous curves screaming for attention. She had a good feeling about today and the first thing she did when she woke up this morning was replay the voicemail Leonard had left her yesterday evening. She realized it could only mean one thing—he was going to take on her case. He had apologized profusely for not keeping their phone consultation appointment yesterday morning due to an unexpected emergency, but all had been forgiven. Naomi was going to have the opportunity to meet him and explain her situation in person.

She unpinned her long silky curls and watched as they bounced against her shoulders. She quickly tamed her flyaways and spruced up her face. After she was done, she headed in the next room to check on her mother.

"Good morning, Ma!" Naomi was surprised to find her mother already propped up in the bed with the television on. While her condition hadn't changed, she was slowly getting her energy back as the days moved on.

"Where are you going all dressed up?"

Naomi walked over to the bed and kissed her mother on the cheek. "I have an appointment with the lawyer. He's going to help me get my babies back." She smiled.

Her mother shook her head.

"What's wrong? I thought we talked about this."

"I don't understand why you wanna go screwing with things. If it ain't broke, don't try to fix it."

Naomi was taken aback. "Exactly whose side are you own?" Naomi stepped back and stared her mother down.

"I'm not on anybody's side, but Charles is a good man and he's done nothing but be a father to his children."

To keep from screaming her head off, Naomi sucked in a deep breath. "A little support would be nice."

Her mother upturned her nose and faced the television.

"I don't know what's wrong with this family. I've done every-thing in my power to prove I'm a better woman than before." She began to tear up. "I've paid for my mistakes and I'm still paying for them. But what I'm not going to do is give up on my children. I had them! Me!" Her pleas seemed to fall on deaf ears.

Her mother finally turned to her. "Well, if you love those boys like you say you do, leave them be with their father. They don't know you anymore…Naomi…Denise…or whoever you are now. You don't get sympathy from me for abandoning your kids!" she said flatly.

With tears streaming down her face, Naomi stood frozen and in shock. "I see," she said as tears clogged her throat. "Well, I'm sorry you feel that way, my dear *perfect* mother." She practically stormed out of the room to go get her things. When she passed her mother's room again, she simply walked right on by, headed straight for the front door, more determined than ever to get her children back.

41

Not even seconds after she had pulled up to her parents' home did Sabrina get a phone call from the hospital notifying her that her husband had been admitted. She was greatly relieved, but fearing the worst, she waited for the nurse to give her more details of what had happened.

"He was brought in about an hour ago with a mild concussion," the woman said. "But he's been stabilized and he's doing fine."

Sabrina exhaled. "That's good to know," she said. "I'm on my way." She had peeled away from the curb and driven straight there.

After having stayed overnight with Luke, they both agreed he was well enough for them to leave.

"We have to hurry up before that detective comes back," Luke said.

"Where are your clothes?" Sabrina asked, frantically searching the room.

Luke pointed to the closet. "Check in there."

Sabrina opened the small closet and retrieved the bag with Luke's clothes in it. She walked back over to the bed and began untying the hospital gown. It pained her to see all the bruises Jeff had left behind. Luke had bruised ribs, cuts, a busted lip, and two swollen black eyes. She wanted to kill Jeff for this.

After getting Luke's clothes on, they slipped out the door and down the hall undetected. She wheeled him onto the elevator and when they made it to the lobby, they ditched the wheelchair and disappeared like two thieves in the night, headed for his brother's.

"How's our baby doing?" Luke asked.

Sabrina looked over at her husband and smiled. "Fine, honey. The baby's doing perfectly fine."

42

"Here are those copies you asked for, Mr. Dupree."

"Thanks, Stacey," Leonard said, looking up from his notepad.

"Would you like a refill on your coffee, Mrs. Adams?"

"No thank you." Naomi smiled.

"How about you, Mr. Dupree?"

"I'm fine as well."

The banker smiled at the two of them and walked back out of the room.

"You must be one of their top customers to receive this type of treatment," Naomi acknowledged.

Leonard chuckled a bit. "Well, let's say the perks come when you're connected." He smiled. "The president of the bank happens to be golfing buddies with my best friend."

"Awww…I see."

"Yeah, I get to use the conference room whenever I need it, and in addition to that, my clients get to be dazzled with a little Southern hospitality." He flashed another knowing smile.

"Well, they do a fine job. I'm sold! Ha, ha, ha."

Leonard took one last look over his notes. "It looks like I have everything I need to get started on your case. So in the meantime, I'll do a little background digging on Charles and his wife—"

"Do we really have to get her involved? She's been so supportive."

"I understand. But it would behoove us to do some fact-checking on her as well. After all, she does live in the same home as Charles and your children."

Naomi took a deep breath. "Okay."

Leonard paused briefly. "Did you have any more questions for me?"

"Nope. I think you've just about covered them all."

He dug in his wallet and handed her a card. "If that's it, we'll be in touch," he said. They both stood up and he extended his hand.

"Thank you," Naomi said. "You have no idea what this means to me."

"It's my pleasure. I look forward to embarking on this journey with you."

They each headed out of the conference room. As they passed the safe deposit box room, Leonard knocked on the first door and said, "I'm done, man."

Naomi walked alongside him, her eyes perusing the lovely branch in the process. Leonard began introducing her to all the other tellers and bankers on their way toward the elevator.

"Where'd you park?" Leonard asked as they stepped on.

"Fifth level," Naomi said.

"Cool. So did I."

Before the elevator door could close, a hand stopped it.

"I…got…the papers," he said.

Leonard nodded as the man passed the folder to him. Naomi bucked her eyes in disbelief. This simply could not be.

"Greg!" she uttered.

He turned around and his eyes widened.

"Na…omi! You…bitch. You…stole my money!" He rushed Naomi and before she knew it, his hands were wrapped around her throat. She fought for air as he choked her out in a death grip.

"Hey, hey, hey!" Leonard plucked Greg's fingers from around

her neck, but it wasn't enough. The moment he was free, Greg came right back at her.

Naomi struggled to breathe through her nose as Greg attacked her viciously.

"Cool it, man!" Leonard said, finally pulling Greg off of her a second time.

Naomi raced out of the elevator once the doors opened. Her face was flushed red and her throat felt like it had been ripped wide open. Tears fell from her eyes as she stared bafflingly at the man she loved.

"What the hell is going on here?" Leonard said, outraged. His voice echoed off the rooftop of the garage.

Naomi could hardly speak. Her breathing grew unsteady as she tried to recover and gain clarity for herself.

"She...took...off with...all my...money!" Greg accused.

Her mouth fell open. "What? You left me and went back to your wife!"

Greg shook his head.

Leonard's eyes darted from one to the other.

"I would have never left you! I love you," Naomi said. "Can we just go somewhere private and talk. I'll tell you everything you need to know."

"First, where...is...my money?"

Naomi wondered why his speech was so slurred. He had never spoken that way before.

"I have it, baby. The money, the house, everything...I have it."

Leonard had a confused look on his face. "Okay, I hate to leave you two lovebirds, but I have a few more errands to run. Are you going to be okay?" he asked Greg.

Greg looked at Naomi who still had tears rushing down her face. He looked down at her ring finger and walked over to where she stood.

"I'll…call…you."

Leonard nodded. "Nice meeting you again…Mrs. Adams." His brows furrowed as he held a slight distrust in his face. Naomi could only imagine what he must have been thinking of her. This surely left a terrible impression.

Embarrassed, she smiled at him and he took off in the opposite direction. She turned to Greg and put her arms around him. "I was worried I would never see you again."

Greg wiped the tears from her eyes and kissed her lightly on the forehead. "It's okay…I'm here now."

They walked hand in hand to her car and drove a short mile down the street to a diner. Naomi was prepared to tell him everything. The entire truth. She only hoped he was ready to hear it.

It hadn't been easy but somehow Naomi managed to get through that conversation. She told him everything there was to tell from how she met his wife, Vivian, in rehab, up to the point where she had been paid to skip town. Naomi and Greg had both been bamboozled by the same woman, only Vivian had not tried to kill her like she had Greg. He poured out every scandalous detail, even how Vivian had staged the scene to look like a suicide. Greg had unloaded a lot, and it all explained why Vivian wanted her to disappear.

"So what are we going to do now?" Naomi asked as she held Greg's hand.

"We're…going to…wait…until the…dust settles," Greg replied. "Then we'll…get her."

Naomi pulled into the Love Field airport. She had purchased Greg's first-class, one-way ticket online and had arranged for a driver to pick him up upon his arrival. He was all set to go and while she hated to see him leave, he needed to go in hiding for a while.

"After I get things situated with my mom and children, I'll be home," she said, teary-eyed.

Greg nodded his head. She hugged him one last time and kissed him on the lips. "I love you."

"I...love you...too, Denise."

She smiled as he embraced her new name. She had worried he would think she was crazy, but this was the change and new beginning that she needed. In a way she was also venerating the dead woman; after all, it was she who had brought them together.

Naomi pressed her lips tightly as tears flowed down her apple cheeks. When Greg went inside the building, she pulled off.

Two hours later, Naomi was in the parking lot of Main Event. She was mentally drained, but she headed inside the huge entertainment arena anyhow. There was no way she was cancelling her plans with her boys.

Naomi checked the time again. Jacquelyn was unusually late. She sat at the bar sipping on a glass of peach tea when she decided to text Jacquelyn that she was at the bar. Maybe they were walking around looking for her. Another fifteen minutes passed and still no word from Jacquelyn or the boys. Worry clouded Naomi's face and as she stood up to leave, the force of gravity knocked her back down.

"Surprised to see me?" Charles asked, taking a seat right beside her.

Naomi looked around in a panic. "Where are my boys?" she spat angrily.

"They're right where they need to be."

Naomi's heart began to race. She couldn't believe that bitch turned on her.

"So you think I'm going to just let you *take* my kids away from me?"

Naomi didn't respond.

"Well, you have another damn thing coming. You will never see them again!" Charles said. He looked down at her beverage. "You haven't changed one bit! You're still the same alcoholic bitch I wish I never met."

"Fuck you!"

"Fuck yourself. And when I thought you couldn't get any dirtier, you try to turn my own wife against me. Yeah, she told me everything, after I confronted her." He shook his head. "Your mother was right."

"My mother?"

"Yeah. She put me on to you two." He smirked. "Woman, I've been one step ahead of you since you've been here. So go ahead and hire all the lawyers you'd like, but I guarantee you, no one, and I do mean *no one*, is gonna take my kids from me. And if you think I'm playing, try me!"

"I *will* get my babies back! Watch me."

"Over my dead body!"

Naomi stood up from the barstool and cut her eyes at him. "Well, if that's what it takes," she admonished, "so be it."

43

The ringing of his cell phone forced him to pause what he was doing and answer it. He had ignored all of her calls from the previous day, up until now. If he ignored this one, she would suspect that something was up.

"Leonard speaking," he answered finally.

"Leonard, have you heard from Greg?" Vivian asked in a panicky tone.

"No, I haven't," he lied. "Not since Wednesday. Why, is everything okay?"

"No! He escaped from Legacy Garden Wednesday night and no one has seen or heard from him since."

"Have you notified police?"

"Not yet. I was hoping he was with you."

"I'm sorry. This is the first time I've heard anything of it."

Vivian grew quiet.

"I'll keep my eyes and ears open. Surely, he'll call one of us," Leonard said, knowing otherwise.

"Please call me as soon as you do hear anything. I'm worried sick something might have happened to him."

"Try not to worry yourself sick, Vivian. We'll find him."

"Thanks, Leonard." She hung up the phone.

Leonard looked at the phone a second longer and briefly exhaled. He had dodged a bullet that was meant for Greg. It had been one helluva month so far and it was a miracle he still had his head on straight. However, he still somehow felt trapped in the middle of Greg and Vivian's fiasco. He had wrongfully doubted his friend, but after hearing Greg's entire side of the story, everything began to make perfect sense as to why Vivian would have wanted her husband dead. Instead of going straight to the authorities as Leonard had advised, Greg decided to hide out. No one knew of his whereabouts except for he and Denise, and he was going to keep it that way.

"Here you are, Mr. Dupree," the young clerk behind the desk said as she passed Leonard the gorgeous, white wedding gown. It was a strapless, opulent trumpet gown with a fitted silhouette and flared hem. It was the perfect dress; it was identical to the one Nadine had already been eyeing. He had found the magazine cut-out a week ago on her nightstand. He had contacted the designer and had it shipped straight to the restaurant. Once it arrived, he took it to Nadine's cleaners to be altered, considering they already had her measurements on file.

Leonard examined the dress and the cathedral-length veil that flowed like a train. He imagined his bride wearing it.

"It's very beautiful. Lucky woman," the clerk said.

"Thank you. For everything."

Leonard gathered the items and took to the door. He thought he could wait until next month to get married, but he could not. With everything that had transpired in the past few weeks, he found himself getting more and more distracted from telling her the truth about his health. He decided that he wasn't going to do this to himself anymore. It was killing him inside, and it was about time he faced his own music. He made up his mind that tonight would be the night he whisked her away, and once they were all alone, he would tell her his innermost secret. Only then would he truly know if their love was real.

44

Nadine loved surprises, so when Leonard called and said that he had a special surprise for her, she couldn't leave work fast enough to find out exactly what it might be.

"You guys have a great weekend!" she called out to her staff jovially.

"You too!" Belinda hollered back. "And don't forget to bring me your Aunt Mickey's peach cobbler recipe. I need it for my Thanksgiving dinner."

"I've made myself a note," Nadine assured her. Balancing her purse and flowers in hand, she made her way to the elevator.

The instant she got in her car, she pulled out her phone to call Jeff. Considering the huge favor she had done for him this week, he owed her this big time.

"Are you at work?" she asked when he answered.

"No. Why, what's up?"

"I was hoping you could pick your son up from daycare."

"Yeah. That's not a problem. Deandra and I were just wrapping up what we're doing here."

"Thank you," she said.

"Everything all right?"

"Everything's great."

"All right, here are those daily worksheets I copied for you," she heard a woman say in Jeff's background. "Remember if you have any questions or if anything changes, you can call me. It was such a pleasure meeting with you and Deandra today. I look forward to seeing the two of you next week. Same time."

"Thanks, Dr. Gilbert. We'll see you then," Jeff replied.

"I hope I'm not interrupting anything." Nadine could hear footsteps descending. She wanted so badly to ask if they were in a therapy session but decided it was none of her business. If he wanted her to know, he would have volunteered the information.

"No, you're good. I've been meaning to discuss something with you, but it can wait another time."

"Okay. Well, I have another call coming through. I'll be by Sunday to get him."

"Sure thing," Jeff said right before she clicked off the line to take Leonard's call.

"Hey, baby." She could barely contain her smile.

"And where exactly is my beautiful bride to be?" he asked.

"I'm en route. About forty minutes until I'll be home."

"Good. I can't wait to see you."

"Neither can I," she said. "So what's all this fancy talk about special weekend plans?"

"Let's just say that I've planned us a nice little getaway trip."

"Well, I like the sound of that."

"I figured you would."

If only he could see how much he had her blushing. She was as giddy as a teenager going out on her first date. She could literally feel the butterflies dancing around in her stomach.

"While I get back to reviewing our itinerary, I need you to make it home safely."

"Yes, sir," she said in her seductive tone.

"See you soon," Leonard said.

Nadine dropped her phone back inside her purse and drove five miles over the speed limit to get home faster. She arrived in record time. When she pulled into the parking lot, she found Leonard loading up the car. She snuck up behind him.

"Boo," she whispered in his right ear. Leonard turned around and gave her a kiss on the lips.

"I've missed you too." He chuckled.

Nadine's smile widened. "Is there anything you need me to do?"

He shook his head. "I've taken care of everything. All I need is your fine body in this car."

Nadine had no idea they were headed to Las Vegas until they had checked their bags at the airport. Yet when the limousine pulled into the private entrance of their luxurious Bellagio villa, she knew right away that this would be a weekend she would never forget. Never in her life had she experienced anything so grand.

"Is this really happening?" she asked Leonard as they walked hand in hand throughout their weekend paradise.

"You better believe it is," he replied, feeding her one of the delicious chocolates situated in a bowl next to a beautiful arrangement of flowers in the foyer.

She nearly melted as her eyes anxiously roamed the European-designed, 6,500 square-foot, two-bedroom villa and its fancy décor. She couldn't imagine the price tag on a room like this.

"Something smells delicious," she said as they headed into the formal dining area.

"Welcome home," the butler greeted with a smile. "Your dinner is being prepared and will be ready shortly."

"Thank you," Leonard said.

Nadine was speechless. This all felt so surreal. They continued their tour of the breathtaking property and all of its finest amenities from a private courtyard with a fireplace, pool, spa, massage room, sauna, fitness center and spacious his-and-her bathrooms. Once they made it to the master bedroom, they stopped to take in the scenery.

"This is so amazing," Nadine said, kissing him.

"I'm glad you approve." He smiled and planted more passionate kisses on her chin, her neck, and her collarbone. Their eyes met again and he cupped her chin between his fingers. "Do you honestly love me enough to spend the rest of your life with me?"

"I love you enough to spend an eternity with you. Before and after life," she said, a sincere smile planted on her face.

He took a deep breath. "Let's make it official. I see no need in waiting anymore. Why put off until tomorrow, what we can do today."

"Are you saying to me what I think you're saying to me?"

"I want to make you an honest woman tonight. That's why I brought you here. I'm ready to make you all mine."

"Yes…yes," she said. "Wait! I don't have a dress. My aunt—" He pressed a finger to her lips to quiet them. He walked right over to the large walk-in closet and came out with her wedding dress. "How…did…you?"

"There's nothing stopping us now," he said with the most handsome smile brushed across his face.

She looked down at her ring finger. "You're right. There's not."

Her nerves were getting the best of her and Nadine did not understand why. This was the moment she had been waiting all of her life for. The moment she had dreamed constantly about.

And now that the time had come, she had wedding jitters. Not once had she ever stopped to question if Jeff was right. Was she jumping in way too fast? Was she about to marry Leonard to get back at Jeff? As she sat in the bathroom pondering over whether or not she was about to make the biggest mistake of her life, her fiancé was patiently waiting on the other side of that door, willing and ready to do what no man had ever asked her to do, and that was make her his wife. He was indeed something special, but why was she second-guessing herself?

"You all right in there, babe?" Leonard called through the door.

Nadine cleared her throat. "Yeah, honey, I'm fine!" she lied. "Just patting on some more makeup!"

"Okay, sweetheart. I'll be waiting in the chapel."

"Okay!" Nadine got up from the chair and walked over to the mirror. She looked exactly as she imagined she would look on her wedding day, even more beautiful. She took a deep breath and said a silent prayer as she lowered the veil over her eyes and made her way back inside the wedding chapel. It was time.

"I now pronounce you husband and wife" were the words that played in Nadine's head.

She couldn't believe her and Leonard had officially tied the knot, and the best thing about it, she felt like it was one of the best decisions she had ever made in her life. She and Leonard sipped on the finest champagne as their limo driver drove them back to their villa to kick off their honeymoon.

"So how do you feel, Mrs. Dupree?"

"Like the luckiest woman in the world," Nadine said, cuddling next to him. They kissed intensely and Leonard began touching her in places he had never ventured to before. Fireworks began to go off inside of her like jolts of electricity causing her panties to get wetter with every touch. She could almost feel her husband's tongue feasting on the swelling flesh between her thighs and driving itself in and out of its candied essence.

"I want you so bad," Leonard confessed, sucking gently on her neck and shoulder.

"And you have me," she replied. The limo came to a slow stroll and that's when the driver called out that they had arrived at the villa. He came around and opened their door, wishing them a lovely honeymoon.

"You betcha we will!" Leonard said, sweeping her up in his arms. He carried her through the villa and into the bedroom where rose petals had been scattered over the floor, leading to the bed. He laid her across the bed next to a bottle of chilling champagne and chocolate-covered strawberries. Nadine took one of the fruit into her mouth while he stared at her like he had never seen anything so exquisite. She propped her head up on one hand and smiled up at him.

"Ready for that *major event?*" She smiled sexily.

"More ready than you'll ever know. But first…first, I have to tell you something."

Nadine lured another strawberry into her mouth. "What do you have up your sleeve now?" she teased playfully, smiling up at him.

Leonard sat on the bed next to her and took her hand into his. He looked down at her ring and kissed it. She sat up completely once a pair of tears began crawling down his face. It was the first time she had ever seen him this emotional.

"What's wrong, baby? Talk to me," she said, rubbing his hand softly.

Leonard pulled in his bottom lip. "Nadine, I'm HIV positive."

She felt like the air had been knocked out of her lungs. Her chest instantly felt constricted and tight and her breathing became labored.

"This is not funny," she managed between breaths.

More tears rolled down his face. "I wish it were not the truth. But I'm sorry, it is."

She shot up from the bed and looked down at him as though merely sitting next to him would cause her to get it as well. "How could you do this to me?" At first it came out in a whisper before she screamed it out. "How could you do this to me?" she yelled, tears rolling down her face.

Leonard stood up and walked toward her, but she backed away.

"I'm sorry," he said. "I wanted to tell you sooner, but—"

"There are no buts! You should have told me on day one!"

"Had I done that and you would have never given me the time of day!"

"And that's my right! My choice! You don't keep something that serious a damn secret!" she shouted. "This is my life you're toying with."

"If you love me like you say you do, my illness should not matter."

"That's so unfair and you know it! This is about the fact that you lied."

"I didn't lie, I just never came out and told you."

"There's no difference in my book. The point is you knew that I would have never agreed to marry you under the circumstances."

"So now the real Nadine surfaces. Didn't those vows mean anything to you?"

"Yeah, they did. But that was before I learned that I had been trapped in a lie."

"Please give us a chance to make this work," he begged. "I love you so much and I never meant to hurt you."

Nadine shook her head as unending tears traveled down her face. "I'm sorry, Leonard." She slipped off her wedding ring. "I can't do it. I can't stay married to you."

"Please don't. I'm begging you. Let's talk this through. We can fix this."

She could barely stand to look at him. "I have to go."

"Don't leave like this."

His words fell to the wayside as she snatched up her purse and belted for the door. She called for service and a limo was there in no time to take her back to the airport. She caught a red-eye flight back to Dallas and was in a cab in less than four hours from leaving Las Vegas.

Nadine paid her fare and tipped the driver before getting out of the car. She had never felt so deceived or cried so much in her entire life. As the driver pulled off, she walked up the driveway, her flowy wedding gown sweeping the asphalt along the way. She was an utter mess, but she didn't care. She rang the doorbell three times before the door finally swung open. Jeff's eyes bucked when he saw who was standing on the other side of it.

"What's going on?" he asked confused. Her tears flowed like a river, obviously telling her story. After quickly looking her over, Jeff's face softened. "Come on in."

Nadine didn't have to say a word. He took her by the hand and led her to his bedroom. Once the door closed, everything they had lost, slowly made its way back to them. They made love like they had never made love before, and for the first time ever, Nadine didn't feel ashamed for doing it. She allowed Jeff's love to numb her pain and dry her tears, even if it was only for one night. They climaxed together one last time and he stroked her face as she lay on top of him, comfortably rocked into a deep sleep.

About the Author

N'Tyse currently juggles her writing career with being a full-time mother, wife, and filmmaker. She is the author of *Twisted Seduction*, *Twisted Vows of Seduction*, and *My Secrets Your Lies;* editor of *Gutta Mamis;* and the executive producer of the documentary film *Beneath My Skin*.

Go beyond the pages and visit the author at:

Website: www.ntyse.com

Facebook: author.ntyse

Twitter: ntyse

Email: ntyse.amillionthoughts@yahoo.com

Fighting the Epidemic

The abbreviation HIV stands for human immunodeficiency virus. It is the virus that can lead to acquired immunodeficiency syndrome, or AIDS. Unlike some other viruses, the human body cannot get rid of HIV. That means that once you have HIV, you have it for life. CDC (Centers for Disease Control and Prevention) estimates that 1,201,100 persons aged thirteen years and older are living with HIV infection, including 168,300 (14%) who are unaware of their infection. Over the past decade, the number of people living with HIV has increased, while the annual number of new HIV infections has remained relatively stable. Still, the pace of new infections continues at far too high a level—particularly among certain groups.

In 2013, an estimated 47,352 people were diagnosed with HIV infection in the United States. Blacks represent approximately 12% of the U.S. population, but accounted for an estimated 44% of new HIV infections in 2010. They also accounted for 41% of people living with HIV infection in 2011. Since the epidemic began, an estimated 270,726 blacks with AIDS have died, including an estimated 6,540 in 2012. The greater number of people living with HIV (prevalence) in African American communities and the fact that African Americans tend to have sex with partners of the same race/ethnicity means that they face a greater risk of HIV infection with each new sexual encounter.

Lack of awareness of HIV status can affect HIV rates in communities. Almost 73,600 HIV-infected people in the African American community in 2011 were unaware of their HIV status. Diagnosis late in the course of HIV infection is common, which results in missed opportunities to get early medical care and prevent transmission to others. The socioeconomic issues associated with poverty—including limited access to high-quality health care, housing, and HIV prevention education—directly and indirectly increase the risk for HIV infection, and affect the health of people living with and at risk for HIV.

Know your status and get tested!

References

www.cdc.gov

www.aids.gov

Where Can I Get Tested?

You can ask your health care provider for an HIV test. Many medical clinics, substance abuse programs, community health centers, and hospitals offer them, too. You can also:

1) Visit National HIV and STD Testing Resources and enter your ZIP code.

2) Text your ZIP code to KNOWIT (566948), and you will receive a text back with a testing site near you.

3) Call 800-CDC-INFO (800-232-4636) to ask for free testing sites in your area.

4) Contact your local health department.

5) Get a home testing kit (the Home Access HIV-1 Test System or the OraQuick In-Home HIV Test) from a drugstore.

References
www.cdc.gov
www.aids.gov

WONDERING HOW IT CAME TO THIS?
GET CAUGHT UP WITH HOW IT ALL STARTED IN

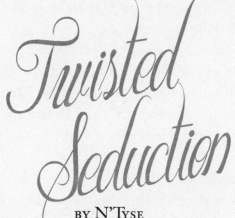

BY N'TYSE

AVAILABLE FROM STREBOR BOOKS

1

Three years earlier

It was so dark and windy that night. Nadine planned on leaving right after choir rehearsal and heading straight home because she had an early morning briefing with Denise, her business partner and best friend, and the rest of their staff. They were going to discuss a strategy to save the $6 million dollar portfolio they were in danger of losing to the bank.

The car alarm to Nadine's Inuit white Audi made a chirping sound when she pressed the keyless entry remote to deactivate it. Just as she got ready to open her door, Jeff Jackson, Denise's husband, appeared out of nowhere with his arm graciously extended in Nadine's direction.

"Here, let me get that for you," Jeff offered, stepping in front of Nadine before she could reach for the door handle. "Woman, you know better than to come out here all by yourself while it's this dark," he playfully chastised.

Nadine worked up a yawn. "Isn't this sacred ground?"

Jeff let out a loose chuckle. "Yeah, but I can tell you right now that doesn't mean anything to a base-head." Jeff was born and raised in the hood and wasn't afraid to face the facts. It was a cruel world and the church they attended just so happened to be located in one of the worst parts of it.

Nadine smiled at Jeff's sincere concern for her safety. She leaned over to place her purse on the passenger seat. The fruity air freshener that hung from the neck of her rearview mirror had the entire car smelling like a watermelon patch. The scent was so strong, Nadine instantly regretted choosing it over the jasmine floral deodorizer she normally bought. She slowly turned back around to face a tower of smooth and handsome dark chocolate. Jeff was well dressed as always, wearing a black, two-button, single-breasted suit jacket; underneath it a white French-fly dress shirt. Blue denim instead of dress pants. Nadine never thought a pair of jeans could look so damn good on a man. She struggled to keep her gaze from settling on Jeff's lower half, allowing her eyes to take in his large white patent leather Jordans; at least a size twelve in her estimation. Not only did Jeff have a natural swagger, he had a sense of style, too. Old school flava with New Age spunk and looks that could conjure the panties right off a woman.

Nadine's eyes hungrily examined him from head to toe. Something was missing and then it hit her at once; his glasses. With the bit of light from her car, she was able to look straight into his mesmerizing chestnut-brown eyes.

"Where's Denise?" she inquired finally. "I thought she'd be here tonight." She pushed her hair behind her ears. It never failed. Every time she found herself in Jeff's presence, she grew nervous. Out of the six years she'd known him, that butterfly feeling still swarmed around the pit of her stomach, holding her accountable for all of her woulda-coulda-shouldas.

Jeff folded his arms. "I don't know where my wife is. She said she needed to take care of some things at the office and then she'd be heading over afterwards, but"—Jeff scoffed as he looked around the empty parking lot—"I guess we can see she never got around to it. So she has me running her errands." He raised a stack of Christmas programs bound together with a thick rubber band. But even if Denise hadn't asked him to drop off the programs, he probably would have volunteered, knowing that Nadine would be here. He relished every chance to see her. He just wished that one day he could work up the nerve to tell Nadine how he'd truly felt about her all these years.

Nadine's furrowed eyebrows showed her suspicion because Denise hadn't mentioned missing rehearsal when they spoke two hours prior. Or maybe Denise had and Nadine was just too tired to re-member. But had Nadine known in advance, she would have con-sidered skipping rehearsal herself. She could barely stay awake. She glanced down at her watch, blinked sleepily.

Jeff tried not to stare at Nadine, but failed terribly. His disobe-dient eyes scanned her 5'8" frame. He was checking all of her out and with God as his witness, Nadine was still the finest woman he'd ever laid eyes on. "So where you heading off to?" he asked, examining her from a new angle.

Nadine's reply was uneven. "I'm headed home. It's so late." She stifled a yawn. "Excuse me. Not only is it past my bedtime, but your wife and I have an early meeting tomorrow with a client that wants us to analyze his accounts. Can you believe that after all the time we spent winning him over, he continues to make us jump through hoops and over hurdles to maintain just a piece of his portfolio?" She shook her head, allowing the frustration that had been lurking all day to show its ugly face. "All the money we made for him and now he's ready to bail out on us. Some people are so damn ungrateful—!" Nadine caught herself, raised her right hand to the sky, bit down on her tongue as a faint smile appeared. "Lord, forgive me. That was so unladylike."

Jeff shook his head, smiled. "Don't worry about it. You must have forgotten that I'm married to a woman that cusses like a sailor. Besides, if something is on your mind, let it off."

Nadine inhaled as much of the polluted night air as she could take in at once. "It's just"—she raised her hands and then dismissed the thought altogether once she felt herself getting worked up again—"Never mind."

Jeff stood directly in front of Nadine, taking in her radiant smile, sexy aura, and the beautiful personality that had first attracted him to her way back when. He often wondered what would have happened between them if he'd confessed to her early on that she was a longing desire he kept tucked in the nest of his heart. He imagined what it would have been like marrying Nadine instead of Denise. He envisioned Deandra, his daughter, having Nadine's brown, narrow eyes, round nose, and smooth butterscotch skin so enticing it was only a fraction away from appearing edible. And since the day they'd first met, he often fantasized about making love to Nadine whenever he was intimate with Denise. He imagined making memories between her legs as she counted backwards from ten, a digit for every inch of his blessings. He fantasized about stroking Nadine so deep that in the middle of her climax she'd call out his name in a cursing fit because he was fucking her so damn good. Then before she could even cross that finish line, he'd deepen his thrust, harden his stroke, grab her by the waist and force her warm erotic passion to surrender to his own as they rode the waves of ecstasy together. Jeff couldn't get Nadine out of his head and the only thing he felt guilty about was the realization he didn't want to. She supplied him with peace and didn't even know it.

"Oh! Have I lost my mind?" Nadine blurted, breaking Jeff's concentration with a smile that exposed straight white teeth shaped by childhood braces. "How could I stand here and not congratulate you on the new promotion? I hear you're running things now, Mr. General Manager." She straightened her posture. "So when I'm out of a job tomorrow," she said, pointing a perfectly manicured finger at herself and then at Jeff, "I'll be running over to your job. Sell a few cars, sweep some floors, hang balloons or something." She laughed. While Nadine was only joking, the weight of her last comment forced her to lean back against her driver door. It was as though she just set off an explosive the way the words ricocheted from her mouth, leaving a terrible aftertaste. The uncomfortable thought of working for anyone other than the extremely wealthy clients who bankrolled her lifestyle was depressing, not to mention a hard pill to swallow. She could never go back to the clock-punching days that barely financed a third of her wardrobe. She could barely eat off of those checks, she remembered painfully. If it hadn't been for the aunt that raised her and put her through school, she didn't know how she would have managed.

Before allowing the threat of losing their most prized client take hold of her, Nadine switched her mindset back to the present. She sucked in her lips. *Now what were we just talking about?* she thought. Finally remembering, she said, "So I guess everybody's *hustling* nowadays to maintain what they have. This recession has really hit us in the financial industry."

Listen to her. Jeff laughed inside at how she carefully pronounced every word. Even when Nadine tried to fit in and speak the lingo, the slang, it just didn't sound right coming out of her mouth. But her attempts were always flattering. "Yeah, everybody's gotta have a back-up plan to stay on top of all this madness," he replied. "But speaking of hustling, Denise and I just got into an argument about that the other day. She thinks I'm working too much overtime, but hell, that was in my job description. She was unhappy with me *just* selling cars. Now that I'm managing the dealership, she's still unhappy."

Nadine's face showed her concern. Denise normally shared everything with Nadine about her marriage, but surprisingly she hadn't mentioned anything to Nadine about this. As far as Nadine knew, Denise was ecstatic about her husband being promoted to general manager; at least proud enough to share the news with the entire staff one day in a board meeting.

"Well, you guys will work it out," Nadine assured him with a questionable sincerity in her voice. She allowed herself a brief pause, then continued. "Seriously, how long have I known you two to go through these periods of being mad over nothing?" She answered for him, her neck moving with each word. "Too long. It must be a marriage thing," she said, shrugging her shoulders, at a loss for a better explanation. Before the sentence left her mouth though, Nadine knew she was lying to Jeff. She tried coaching herself on the next best thing to say until she saw the look of unhappiness swell in his eyes. What had she gotten herself into now? Jeff and Denise's marriage wasn't any business of hers, she kept telling herself, and it would only complicate things if she stood there and allowed him to express himself in a way that made Denise look like a foolish woman undeserving of a good man. Because that would open up doors. Doors she knew should remain closed.

The wind sent another invasive chill and, instantly, Nadine's nipples hardened into bullets as thick as her pinky. The swell of her breasts made the silver, buttoned-down blouse she wore dislodge itself from the waist of her pencil skirt. That should have been her cue to leave but instead she reached in her car, started the engine, and permitted the heat to circulate between them.

Jeff stared into thin air, then back at Nadine. "I just don't know sometimes." He tilted his head. "It's like whatever I do, it's just not good enough anymore," he exclaimed honestly. He couldn't figure out where he'd gone wrong in their relationship but it was apparent that Denise was so wrapped up in herself and everything else that he didn't even exist in her world. That was why it was so easy for him to put in fifty to eighty hours a week and not feel missed at home. When Denise did decide to throw the shit up in his face, it was right before they became intimate. But Jeff was no fool. He knew that it was just another lame ass excuse to keep him from bothering her for sex. So before the night was up, they would be screaming and shouting, then to the couch he would go to finish himself off alone. There was nothing about their marriage that felt special anymore; nothing that gave him a reason to come home every night or a reason to remain faithful. Everything leading up to the point he was at now had been a living hell. And while the pussy coupons women threw his way should have been the quick fix he needed, they did absolutely nothing for him. His only true interest was in one woman—Nadine Collins.

Nadine couldn't help but wonder where all Jeff's complaining was coming from. It was all so sudden, and not that she minded being a listening ear, tonight was just not a good night for it. She had no choice but to refuse to listen to his gripes about Denise, because she was already yawning and struggling to keep her eyes open, and also struggling to keep them from drifting down to the fly of his jeans. That may have actually been the bigger struggle. Oh how she wished just for one second that she had X-ray vision. She moved closer to him.

"Jeff, honey, I want you to try to relax," Nadine said in her calmest voice. She began rubbing his shoulders. He was tense, almost as tense as the muscles in her pussy. She focused on those stubborn knots, massaging her fingers deeply in and out of every groove. Before she knew it, she had gotten herself wet. She looked around the parking lot, which thankfully was now empty except for Jeff's black BMW parked in the far corner under a leaning thirty-foot elm tree. She didn't want to risk someone coming out of the church and seeing the two of them alone.

Jeff tried to loosen up under Nadine's irresistible touch. He didn't want her to feel sorry for him, or maybe he did. He wasn't sure what he wanted Nadine to feel. As long as he had her attention, he was content. "Nothing I do is good enough anymore," he went on to say. "All Denise does is nag. It's like she creates reasons to be pissed at me. And do you know how long it's been since we had sex? Y'all are girls so I know y'all talk about it." If Nadine didn't know, he was about to enlighten her. "Three months! She tell you that?" Jeff held up three stiff fingers. "Not one, not two, but three!"

Nadine stood wide-eyed and fully awake now. She had no idea all of this was happening, and right under her nose because Jeff was absolutely right; she talked to Denise about almost everything. No subject was off limits. At least that's how it used to be.

"Please, help me understand how a woman just loses the desire to be with her man," Jeff said. "Her husband." He stared at Nadine's face, studying her facial response like an open book test. "I mean, come on. Help a brother out. What is she thinking? Is she seeing somebody? You can tell me." He scratched at the coal black waves in his Caesar haircut. "I'm just not getting this shit right now."

Nadine didn't know what to do or say but she could both empathize and sympathize because she wasn't getting any loving either. She'd been celibate for what felt like a decade. Celibate after her last fling had given her crabs, had her rushing to the hospital like a damn fool for believing his two-timing ass when he told her he wasn't seeing anyone else. Since then she vowed to refrain from sex until the timing was right. She'd been so engulfed in work lately she hadn't had the time or patience to date. Besides, in her book, most men were dogs and she refused to waste the time and energy searching for Mr. Right when she had Mr. Right Quick tucked away safely in her bedside nightstand.

"Jeff, I think you really need to talk to your wife about all this. I mean"—Nadine's eyes widened as she flipped both her hands over—"don't you think Denise is the one that needs to hear everything that you're telling *me?*" She hoped she wasn't being hypocritical by saying so.

"Nadine, Denise and I have had the talk a thousand times. It's come to the point where it's pointless with her. She ain't hearing me." He sounded like a man out on his last limb. Speaking with no certainty, hope, or faith for a future with Denise as husband and wife. He could feel the wrinkles in his forehead beginning to form naturally like they've done throughout the course of his marriage. He often wondered if they were permanent lines of love, hate, and unhappiness that would one day interfere with the man whom he had set out to be.

"Maybe I'm just asking for too much. I bet that's it. Where is the woman that doesn't mind if her man is the main breadwinner, the head of the household, the father to their children, and her lover when it's time to be?" Jeff shook his head and took a deep breath. "I guess it's silly of me to think such a woman exists. Hell, I shouldn't have to be in competition with my wife!"

Jeff's titanium wedding band shone like a knight's armor even in the darkest hour. This symbolic piece of jewelry made its statement so loud and clear that Nadine had to avert her eyes. She forced back a silent jealousy that nearly washed up the day's dinner; now a little apprehensive about carrying on the rest of their conversation. Her ears drew themselves to the sound the leaves made as they rustled across the pavement. Maybe the leaves' efforts to escape from their original habitat was Nadine's second cue to get the hell up out of here herself. But while there were so many reasons she needed to turn around and leave, there was only one that kept her standing on her feet with her heated pussy inviting itself into their conversation.

"Jeff, I really wish I could stay and talk about this with you, but, I don't think I'm the most suitable person to give you relationship advice. I don't even have a man myself." She smiled, hoping the gesture would save her from continuing the chat. She didn't feel it was appropriate to discuss Denise's bedroom drama with Jeff. Something about it didn't sit well, but she couldn't deny that being in Jeff's company felt so damn good. His conversation made her moist. Tempted her in ways she didn't realize she could be tempted. Mind-fucked her thoughts so deeply she was on the verge of having a mental climax, if that were even possible.

Nadine snatched her mind out of the gutter. They were just talking. No harm in just talking, she told herself. "What I mean is," she continued, "or I can only assume, that men and women go through periods where they stop…" She was silenced before she could complete her sentence. Jeff leaned in, halting her with a kiss so passionate and so intense. She lifted her hands in the air, trying with little success to avoid touching his body. Fearful that once in his embrace she wouldn't be able to let him go…